IT WAS NOT BUSINESS THAT CHARLES MONTGOMERY WAS WORRIED ABOUT.

This hollow dread that had been building inside him was not due to the complicated administration of the diverse holdings of M.G., Inc. It was his family. It was his wife, Judith, and her hidden tears.

Another door slammed and he heard a furious cry from Jennifer. With a sigh he slowly pushed away from his gleaming rosewood partners desk and stood up. He had planned this miserable trip, so they might as well get going. If it took the whole week he was going to straighten out his two troublesome kids and get to the bottom of Judith's tears. He hadn't busted his butt all this time for nothing. They were sitting pretty now, with everything a family could want. There was no reason for any of them to be unhappy.

But the Montgomerys *were* unhappy. Nothing short of a miracle could hold them together. Yet the most magical things happen at Christmastime. And this year, a miracle is about to find the Montgomerys . . .

Praise for Rexanne Becnel and her novels:

THE ROSE OF BLACKSWORD:

"A medieval tale that activates your imagination with its action and earthy sensuality. Superb!"

—*Rendezvous*

THIEF OF MY HEART:

"Charming . . . this steamy battle-of-wills romance will tug at your heart and keep you turning the pages as fast as you can. Rexanne Becnel is a wonderful talent with a strong, unique voice. Sensual."

—*Romantic Times*

"From the endearing verse on the first page to the final scene . . . this one fulfills every woman's fantasy while sustaining the sensuality of the well-developed characters. Superbly crafted."

—*Rendezvous*

MY GALLANT ENEMY:

"A love story of old to thrill and delight. Much intrigue and an awesome, arrogant, but lovable hero and the lady who turned his heart upside down."

—*Affaire de Coeur*

"Sensitive, realistic and passionate, *My Gallant Enemy* is a delicious medieval love story. Rexanne Becnel is sure to take her place in the ranks of well-loved medieval romance writers."

—*Romantic Times*

Also by Rexanne Becnel:

THE ROSE OF BLACKSWORD

THIEF OF MY HEART
winner of the *Romantic Times* Award
for Best Southern Historical Romance

MY GALLANT ENEMY
winner of the
Waldenbooks' 1991 First Time Romance Author
Award and winner of the *Romantic Times* Award
for Best Medieval Romance by a New Author

Rexanne Becnel

Christmas Journey

A DELL BOOK

Published by
Dell Publishing
a division of
Bantam Doubleday Dell Publishing Group, Inc.
666 Fifth Avenue
New York, New York 10103

ISBN: 0-440-21317-7

Printed in the United States of America

Published simultaneously in Canada

December 1992

10 9 8 7 6 5 4 3 2 1

RAD

To my parents

Rosemary Barcelona and Clifford Rex Chauvin

with love

A special thank-you to my own guardian angels

Audrey Brimmer, GOHS '68

Gurney Nelson, D.R.'s best friend

Sophie Roshefsky Kahn, JCC '91

Chapter One

"It's a hell of a thing when your own family turns on you," Charles Montgomery muttered as he tossed his wife's California French garment carrier and pullman bag into the roomy interior of the car trunk. His face was set in a deep scowl as he thrust a box of expensively wrapped gifts to the side and settled the two Grey-Rose Tapestry bags in place.

"Here." Alexander shoved his amplifier forward, letting it thud onto the smaller pullman case.

"Don't do that!" Charles jerked the amplifier out and set it heavily on the ground. "You don't need that stupid thing, and I'll be damned if I'm going to listen to all that noise for the next week. We're going to the mountains for peace and quiet!"

"Just 'cause *you* want peace and quiet . . ." Alex muttered under his breath.

"Charles, please calm down." Judith Montgomery came down the shallow granite steps toward the car parked within the porte cochere beside the house. "You can't expect this week to be pleasant if you begin it this way."

Charles bit back the retort that rose to his lips, but it was not due so much to the truth of her words as it was to the expression on her face. She had been crying. Despite the beautifully made-up face, the chic outfit, and the perfectly styled hair, he could tell she'd been crying. More and more these days that had become the case, and though he could not understand the reasons for her unhappiness, he nonetheless knew it was real. He forced a smile to his face.

"I'm calm. Don't worry, I'm calm." Then his gaze flickered to Alex. "But I doubt I'll stay calm if I'm bombarded with ear-splitting noise all week. Chances are slim to nothing that Rogers's damn mountain house has a soundproof basement like ours."

Judith placed her vanity case in the trunk, then turned to her fifteen-year-old son, who already towered over her. "Alex, certainly you could survive a week without your guitar and amp." She stared at his sullen, obstinate face, so like his father's. "Or perhaps you could bring just the guitar."

"What's the point?" The boy sent his father an angry look, but he was not outwardly rude to his mother. "An electric guitar without an amp is useless. It's like Dad's car and his car phone. He wouldn't know how to drive if he wasn't talkin' on his stupid car phone!"

At just that moment, Jennifer rushed down the steps wailing as if her heart were broken. Charles shot Alex an aggrieved look, muffling an expletive under his breath as he turned toward his unhappy daughter.

"Now what?" he exclaimed in irritation, then sighed when Jennifer turned away from him and ran into her mother's outstretched arms.

"Jenny? What in heaven's name?"

"Clarisse decided to have a party," the twelve-year-old sobbed onto her mother's shoulder. "Everyone's going to be there. Cliff. Jeremy. Nick. Even Brett." She lifted her face to shoot her father a pained look. "Brett Franklin will be there, but I won't! And all because Daddy wants to go to the dumb mountains!"

Judith's gaze was a mirror of their daughter's. Then she looked away from Charles. "Now, Jenny. Surely there will be other parties."

"No, there won't." The girl sniffled as if the world were truly coming to an end. "Not for me. Sara Smythe has a major crush on Brett, and Clarisse says he kinda likes her too. By the time we get back, they'll be going out. I just know they will!"

"Twelve years old is too young to be going out." Judith tried to soothe her daughter as she pushed a lock of hair back from her wet cheek.

"Babies in love," Alex mocked, poking his forefingers in his cheeks and making a face.

"Mom!"

"Alex," Judith reproved.

In the midst of this chaos a phone jangled sharply. Recognizing the ring of the private business line in his study, Charles hurried up the steps before the housekeeper could come to summon him. As he strode into the house, he determinedly shut out the all-too-familiar pandemonium that was his family life.

In the quiet study he lifted the phone. "Montgomery here."

"Charles. I'm glad I caught you."

At the sound of his longtime business partner's voice, Charles sat back in his big leather chair. "Hey, don't worry about calling me if you have to, Doug. Once we leave the house you can get me on the car phone. And I gave you the number at Rogers's mountain house."

Doug grunted. "Cora pitches a fit if we take the car phone on family trips. Calls that phone my mistress." He laughed. "She says I can have both of them, wife and mistress, but not at the same time. Anyway, back to business. It's Garrington. His wife was recently appointed to the board of the Neighborhood Preservation Center, and now he's not so gung ho about approving our demolition permits for Greenmont."

"Have you reminded him about the considerable contributions we made to his last campaign?"

"You think I'm a fool? Of course I did."

"And promised more of the same?"

"Naturally. Damn," Doug swore in frustration. "This could screw up everything. It's a close enough vote that we need to be sure of him."

Charles was calm and thoughtful. He rubbed his chin slowly with one finger as he stared up at the deep coffers in the ceiling. "Garrington's wife is a Morrison, as I recall. Daughter to Judge William

Morrison and sister to Fred Morrison. That's Morrison Windows, Inc. Maybe if we invited them to bid on the windows for the high-rise, she might be more amenable to our project. Or at least not hostile."

"Morrison Windows? I'll be damned! Where do you get this stuff?"

Charles laughed out loud, already certain the little obstacle Garrington presented was well on its way to being solved.

Doug laughed too. "If there's still any doubt in Garrington's mind, I'll tell him we can get him a fur coat real cheap to give to his wife for Christmas. That ought to ease the pain of losing a few tenement buildings. No, wait. Better make it jewelry. Diamond earrings or the like. Some women are opposed to wearing fur coats, but no woman I've ever known is opposed to diamond earrings."

"You've got that right," Charles agreed, relaxing now.

"I hope you got Judith something expensive for Christmas. Haven't seen much of her at the office lately, but Cora says she's looking a little down in the mouth."

Charles sobered at once, and a crease appeared between his eyes. "We just need a little time away. That's what this trip is for. She'll be smiling again by New Year's. Meanwhile, let me know how it goes with Garrington and his wife."

"Sure thing. Have a good trip. I'll see you in a week."

"Yeah. Keep in touch no matter what."

Charles sat several minutes after he hung up the phone. He heard the house phone ring and Jennifer's rapid footsteps as she ran to get it. He heard Alex's voice raised once in an indecipherable shout, and then a door slammed. But he continued to sit there. Doug would handle Garrington. And if Doug couldn't, then he would call Charles in. No matter what happened, he'd only be a phone call away. There was no reason to worry about business.

But it was not business he was worried about. This hollow dread that had been building inside him wasn't due to the complicated administration of the diverse holdings of M.G., Inc. It was his family. It was Judith and her hidden tears. Only they were no longer hidden so well. When had they begun? he wondered. And why had he never noticed before now?

He sighed and ran a hand through his sandy-colored hair and rotated his head, trying to relax the tense muscles of his neck and shoulders, but it didn't help. On the desk he spied a picture of his family. It had been taken in the hospital, the day Jennifer was born. Alex had been three. Charles picked up the picture and stared hard at it.

Although Judith wore no makeup in the picture, and her hair was barely combed, she looked beautiful. She was smiling at him, not the camera. He and little Alex, who was sandwiched between his mother and father, had been smiling down at baby Jennifer. But Judith had been smiling at him.

It was his very favorite picture of his wife, and though she'd often suggested other photos for his desk, he'd always preferred this one. She looked so happy in it. They *had* been happy that day, he recalled. With the birth of their daughter after a long, troubled pregnancy, his whole life had seemed perfect.

Charles placed the picture back on the desk.

They'd come so far in the past twelve years. His business had soared since then. Yet they weren't nearly so happy. And now . . . And now he couldn't seem to do anything right with Judith anymore.

Their last fight, she'd actually accused him of loving his work more than he loved her, more than the kids. Though her notion was absolutely ridiculous, he couldn't ignore the fact that she seemed to believe it. She believed it, and those damned interfering biddies from that women's group she'd joined believed it, too. How was he supposed to fight them off?

Another door slammed and he heard a furious cry from Jennifer. With a sigh he slowly pushed away from his gleaming rosewood partners desk and stood up. He had planned this miserable trip to the Adirondacks, so they might as well get going. If it took the whole week he was going to straighten out his two troublesome kids and get to the bottom of Judith's tears. He hadn't busted his butt all this time for nothing. They were sitting pretty now, with everything any family could want. There was no reason for any of them to be unhappy.

By the time the big Mercedes reached cruising speed on the interstate, Jennifer had stopped sniffling. Alex was no longer making snide remarks about crybabies, and Judith was gazing through the front windshield instead of pointedly staring out the side window.

"Rogers said there's a stock of firewood at the mountain house," Charles began with a forced air of cheerfulness. "And we can cut down our own Christmas tree."

"Did you remember our presents?" Jennifer asked resentfully from the backseat.

"Yes, dear," Judith answered, still staring straight ahead.

"What about Christmas decorations?" Her voice held a challenge, as if she hoped to catch her parents in a moment of forgetfulness.

Charles answered. "Rogers said there are ornaments in a big box in the basement." He glanced at his daughter's angry face in the rearview mirror. "We'll have everything we need for the best Christmas ever."

"Maybe you will, but I won't. I can't go to Clarisse's party," Jennifer pouted. Charles's hands tightened on the wheel in exasperation, but he refused to be drawn into the debate.

Judith sighed. "I know her party meant a lot to you, Jenny. But there will be other parties."

"Not like this one."

"How about if you have a party? Maybe for Valentine's Day."

Jennifer sat very still in the backseat. "That's too long away. How about New Year's?"

"Remind me to spend the night somewhere else," Alex muttered. He put on his earphones and turned on his Walkman.

Jennifer made a face at him, then leaned toward her mother. "We could do it New Year's and everyone would come."

"I suppose so."

"And we could have a DJ. And I could get a new dress. Oh, and we could have pizzas brought in—" She unfastened her seat belt and hitched her arms over the back of her mother's seat. "You promise I can have this party? You won't change your mind?" She shot a suspicious look at her father.

Judith sighed once more. "I promise, Jenn. Now, please, sit back and put your seat belt on. You know how I feel about seat belts."

"Yes!" Jennifer exclaimed, throwing herself back onto the seat with an excited squeal. "It'll be the best party *anybody's* ever been to—especially better than Clarisse's." She subsided after that, happily contemplating plans for her own party.

As the car headed north, through Westchester County and beyond, to the promise of open spaces in upstate New York, Charles heaved a relieved sigh. Jennifer was taken care of. Now he only had to worry about Alex and Judith. He glanced at his wife, hoping to coax a smile from her. But she was once again staring out the side window. Frustrated even more, he gritted his teeth. With two stabbing motions he turned the car radio on, then set the search mode in action. When the familiar strains of Bing Crosby singing "White Christmas" came on, he gripped the wheel harder with both hands.

"Anyone want to sing along?" He forced himself to sound jovial. He caught a glimpse of Alex in the rearview mirror, but he realized at once that Alex's bobbing head was not nodding agreement. He was only keeping rhythm with the music plugged into his ears. Naturally. But there had been a time—

Charles refused to let himself get maudlin. No doubt every little kid had appeared at least once in a Christmas pageant dressed as an angel or some other appropriate character. Then, just like Alex, they'd turned into incomprehensible teenagers.

Still, the image of Alex dressed in one of his dad's oversized T-shirts and his mother's pale blue robe would not go away. His silver foil wings and halo had wobbled precariously as the trio of angels had scooted onto the stage, and at first he and Judith had feared Alex would forget the words to the song the angels were supposed to lead. But once the music teacher had begun to play the piano, Alex's fearful expression changed. For those few minutes he had been truly angelic, singing at the top of his lungs, louder than anyone else.

"Away in a Manger." That song was meant to be sung by children, Charles decided with a faint smile. Even little Jennifer, who'd been but four at the time, had begun to sing from her position on her mother's lap.

There had been tears in Judith's eyes that night. Tears of happiness.

What he wouldn't give to see that look in her eyes again.

The sharp electronic ring of the car phone pulled him sharply back to the present.

"Montgomery here—Jude, could you turn off the radio?" he asked from the corner of his mouth. "Hello? Yeah, Doug. What gives?"

He shot Judith an encouraging smile as she bent forward to turn off the mellow tones of the Christmas classic, but she didn't meet his gaze. For a moment he lost track of what Doug was saying—something about the delivery of copper piping and one of the unions' position on imports from the Far East.

"—are you there?" Doug's demand pierced through Charles's preoccupation.

"Yeah, yeah. Uh, just bull your way through, Doug. The union's talking big, but those guys are not about to stand tough. Not with jobs like ours so few and far between these days. And the last thing the union can afford is for its own people to scab. No, it's all a bluff. Mark my words."

When he hung up the phone he glanced again at Judith, but this time she was leaning back against the headrest, her eyes closed. He turned the radio back on, hoping that might spark her interest. But Judith did not respond, and as they sped north through the wintry New York landscape, past the suburban tracts, then the farms, and on up into the hills beyond, his heart slowly took on the same icy cast as the world outside the big car. He wasn't sure his plan was going to work. But if it didn't . . .

Charles refused to think about that. He was a master at closing a deal. He always had been. He would simply have to rise above his emotions and do whatever it took.

The sky grew grayer. The clouds pressed closer to the earth. On the radio Elvis Presley sang "Blue Christmas."

With a vicious jab of one finger Charles silenced the singer in mid-sentence. A blue Christmas. He was not a man who believed in omens, but for that moment, at least, he feared the song might be truly prophetic.

The leaden sky stretched north into the mountains, heavy, gray, and threatening. Yet Judith decided it was no more grim than the somber atmosphere in the car. Charles drove in silence. To her relief he had switched off the radio some time ago. The forced cheerfulness of the Christmas music had been only irritating today, as if it were somehow as false as everything else about this trip.

She sighed but deliberately kept her eyes closed. If she appeared to sleep he would not initiate any conversation. It was a cowardly tack, she knew. But she simply was not up to conversation. In the backseat Jennifer had apparently fallen asleep. All that could be heard was the faint hum from Alex's headphones. She hoped the volume wasn't so high as to damage his hearing.

When the car slowed a bit she automatically opened her eyes. In front of them was a brightly painted van, yellow with a wooden rear bumper and a fringed curtain bobbing in the back window.

"Come on," Charles muttered, frowning at the slower vehicle. Passing was not easy on the two-lane state highway, for it twisted and turned over and around the hills. He edged their car nearer the center line and peered past the van. Three cars zipped by heading south. Then a fourth. At once he pressed down on the accelerator, and with hardly a lurch the sedan roared past the other vehicle.

"Damn road hogs," she heard him mutter. Then he glanced at her and caught her watching him. For a long moment their eyes locked, before he had to look back at the road. Then he glanced at her again, a smile firmly in place—his salesman's smile, she realized.

"Not too much farther, Jude. Maybe fifteen miles to Ruddington."

It was Judith who looked away this time. His determined effort to make everything seem all right suddenly tore at her heart. How could she, who had so much—much more than she'd ever hoped for—still be so unhappy? What was wrong with her?

"We can stop there for groceries," Charles continued. "We might as well stock up on everything we need. Did you make a list? Don't forget, we'll need soap and shampoo and toilet tissue, too. Not just food. Though God knows, we'll need plenty of food, too, the way these kids put it away."

"How would you know how much they eat?"

Judith was sorry for her bitter words as soon as they were said. She had resolved to be as pleasant as possible during their trip together. Her outburst the previous week still haunted her; she had vowed there would be no repeat of it. Yet here she was, sharp and accusing when he was trying so hard.

"Dammit, Judith, that's not fair! You act as though I'm a stranger to my own kids—"

He broke off abruptly when Jennifer shifted in the backseat. He kept his eyes on the road ahead, but Judith saw his knuckles whiten as his hands clenched the steering wheel. Once more her eyes closed and she had to swallow a painful lump in her throat.

"I'm sorry, Charles. That was uncalled for."

He didn't answer. For the next fifteen miles only the buzz of unidentifiable music from Alex's headphones broke the hum of the heavy engine—that and the troubled thoughts tumbling through Judith's head. They passed nineteen more vehicles: one tractor trailer, three pickup trucks, four sports cars, two station wagons, two vans, and seven sedans. Did the people in all those cars dread the Christmas holidays as much as she did? Judith wondered. She doubted it.

If only she could explain it to Charles. If only she could explain it to herself. Even in her roundtable group some of the women did not completely understand. Her husband did not mistreat her. He'd never raised a hand to her or the children. He was a good provider and he'd never been unfaithful.

Perhaps it would be easier if he had, she thought bitterly. A woman she could fight. A mistress she could deal with. But what chance had she against the very thing that gave Charles his greatest joy? He was a man who thrived on a challenge. A man obsessed with success. And no one could deny that Charles Montgomery was a success. From a nothing business in a spare bedroom he'd developed M.G. Construction into a tremendous conglomerate, flying in the face of economic slumps, recessions, and the near failure of the construction industry in the mid-eighties. He was touted in business magazines, praised by politicians, and even studied at one local business college.

But the success had not come without cost, at least in Judith's opinion. Oh, they lived in a wonderful house now, in the best neighborhood. The children went to the finest private schools and none of them wanted for a thing. But there had still been a price to pay. The day Charles had announced that Judith need no longer work in the office stood out in her mind. A part of her had been pleased. It was difficult working and taking care of an active toddler. When she'd become pregnant again shortly thereafter, Charles's decision had seemed even more logical. But she hadn't wanted to quit working. Not really.

So she'd started to dabble in decorating, working with the interior designers both for the buildings Charles built as well as the several homes he constructed for them. One house after another, each one bigger and better than the last, in a finer and more exclusive neighborhood.

Charles had even offered to set her up in her own specialty furniture business, with a showroom in one of his developments, and warehouses in an industrial park nearby. But she'd said no. Even now his offer caused an unreasoning spurt of anger in her. He was being generous but she'd been unable to bear it.

So she'd started doing charity work alongside other well-to-do women. But now even that was subject to Charles's manipulations. Was this one's husband/brother/father of any use to M.G., Inc.? Were they politically connected?

She stared out at the depressing brown scenery blurred by the car's speed on the twisting roadway. Charles's answers to her complaints were always the same. His reactions to their arguments never varied. A huge pearl cluster ring. An amethyst bracelet. Diamond earrings. He was happy and therefore he could not recognize that she was not. He was successful, respected, and very wealthy. What more could a person want?

The answer to that question continued to elude Judith. She was by association also a success, respected and rich. But she was not happy and didn't know how to be.

The worst part was that now, when Charles seemed finally to be noticing her dissatisfaction, she was ready to give up. She'd not intended to bring up the idea of divorce. But when he'd accused her of complaining about nothing, she'd exploded. Was divorce nothing? she'd yelled.

They'd made up, of course. She'd cried; he'd apologized; and then they'd made love. But the word, once said, would not leave Judith's consciousness. They'd gone on as normal on the surface, but the idea of divorce had stayed with her.

It was not that she wanted to be rid of Charles. It was more that she wanted to find herself. That concept, of course, was ridiculous in Charles's eyes. She knew that without even discussing it. He was not a man given to introspection, nor did he put any faith in psychology. That was for crazy people, and they were not crazy.

But Judith had felt more and more as if she were heading in that direction. As they drew nearer their Christmas destination, she had to steel herself for the days to come. For the children's sake she must maintain her calm. For Charles's sake also, for she could not begrudge him this appearance of a perfect Christmas, which he wanted so badly.

But what was she to do for herself? For her own sake?

Jennifer woke up as soon as they turned into the packed-gravel parking lot of the Ruddington General Store. Only four other cars were there, and from the looks of the place it was not likely to carry a very large variety of food. What had that banker, Rogers, gotten them into? Judith fumed. First an isolated cabin, and now this ramshackle affair.

"Well, kids," Charles announced as he turned off the car and twisted to look at the pair, a determined smile on his face. "My money says this place started as a trading post in the wilderness. Maybe there are still beaver skins stacked up for sale."

"Beaver skins? Ugh! That's disgusting," Jennifer replied, making a face. She pushed her tangled hair out of her face and stretched.

"Watch it, dork." Alex shoved her outstretched arm back to her own side of the car. "The only thing disgusting around here is you."

"You mean *you*," Jennifer snapped, yanking the base of his earphones from his Walkman. "Too bad there's no Indians around here to scalp you. 'Course even they wouldn't want that rat's nest you call hair

—stop it!" she cried as he grabbed at her hair and yanked hard. "Mom!"

Judith gritted her teeth. "Would you two please stop—"

"Shut up, the both of you!" Charles roared. He glowered at his two children. "If this is the way you're going to behave the whole week—" He broke off but Alex seemed determined not to let things lie. As if he'd been nursing his grievances the entire silent journey, he turned a sullen glare on his father.

"If this is the way we're gonna act the whole week you might as well turn around and go home. Right?"

Judith saw Charles's face darken, but she grabbed his arm before he could react. "Everybody is a little grumpy right now. Let's get out and do our shopping. Do you kids want a soft drink?"

Beneath her hand she could feel his tension, but she only tightened her grasp until he looked away from Alex and met her imploring eyes. Then he sighed.

"Fine. Let's go inside. But not you," he added, glaring at Alex. "You can just stay in the car alone. Maybe then you'll appreciate the company of others a little better."

Judith knew better than to intercede on Alex's behalf. She knew from experience that her interference only made things worse. But why must he always antagonize his father so? It wasn't as if they spent that much time together. Alex could make his own life so much easier if he would just meet his father halfway. But Judith knew that would never happen. Alex was too much like Charles, though neither father nor son would ever admit it. Both of them smart and driven. Both of them determined never to back down and always to get their own way.

She pulled down the vanity mirror and checked her hair, then pulled a lipstick from her Gucci bag and freshened her makeup. But no amount of powder would erase the lines of tension around her mouth, or the faint circles beneath her eyes. Frowning, Judith snapped the visor back into place.

"Give me the mirror, Mom," Jennifer demanded as she began to brush her hair.

"Don't fling your cooties this way," Alex muttered at his sister.

Jennifer ignored him. She clearly knew she'd won the last go-round, and only smiled smugly into the mirror her mother handed her. When she had her bangs arched over her brow just so, she flung the mirror onto the front seat and got out of the car.

"Want me to bring you a root beer?" she asked sweetly, bending slightly to see her brother on the backseat. "Maybe an Almond Joy?" Then her face turned taunting. "Well, too bad!" She slammed the door as hard as she could.

"That was unnecessary," Judith rebuked her as she, too, stepped out of the car. But Jennifer bounded ahead to where her father waited on the unpainted porch of the general store, and Judith wasn't sure she'd heard.

If Alex was like his father, was Jennifer like her? she wondered as she walked up to the store. Did she taunt Charles whenever an opportunity presented itself as Jenny invariably taunted Alex? Up till now she would not have thought so, but how else could she describe her behavior today? She was unhappy, and it appeared she wanted Charles to be unhappy too. She'd given up on believing they could ever be happy again.

Charles had not, though. That was apparent in everything he'd done and said in the last week. But that knowledge only stoked the simmering anger she'd suppressed so long. She knew it was hopeless; why must he be so determined to prove her wrong?

Judith ran her hand nervously down the front of her cashmere blazer, straightening one of the gold medallion buttons before she mounted the steps to join Charles. He had one arm draped about his daughter's shoulders, but Jenny shrugged out of his embrace as her mother approached.

"Be sure to get diet Coke, Mom. Not regular."

"You drink too many soft drinks," Charles said. "Juice would be better for you." When she did not respond but only pulled the door open and entered to the accompaniment of several jingling bells, he turned toward Judith.

"She drinks too many soft drinks," he repeated. "They both do."

Judith shrugged. "You drink too much coffee."

"I'm not a growing child, Jude. There's a difference."

She walked into the small store, past the door he held open for her. "As long as they do things—eat things, or whatever—in moderation, there's no harm done."

"I'd like us to eat good, old-fashioned food this week. Real breakfasts with pancakes and juice. Soups. Stews."

Once more resentment flared in Judith's chest. "I suppose you're cooking?" She yanked a small wire shopping cart from a line of them and headed down one aisle, oblivious to the foods she passed.

Charles hurried to match her brisk pace. "I can make pancakes."

"And soups? And stews?" She stopped abruptly before a display of red-and-white Campbell's soups. Without bothering to examine the labels she began grabbing the cans, then moved a little distance down the aisle to snatch up several cans of Dinty Moore stews.

At that moment Jennifer rounded the corner ahead of them. "No video games. Hardly *any* magazines. But they do have diet Coke." She heaved two six-packs into the cart. "We need some cookies, too."

"How about fruit?" Charles interjected. "You don't eat enough fruit."

Jennifer shot him an aggrieved stare. "Fine, Dad. Get fruit." Then she turned away toward a display of small, individually wrapped desserts.

Judith moved on to the dairy case and added a gallon of milk to the cart. Charles added two more gallons.

"Do you think we could have a turkey on Christmas? Maybe with chestnut stuffing?"

This time it was not anger Judith felt, but a sudden and inexplicable sorrow. Charles wanted a picture-perfect Christmas, complete with happy children, contented wife, and all the traditional trappings. If they played the role, he was convinced they could become that smiling Norman Rockwell family. She, of course, knew better. But as she stood there in the wood-ceilinged store—as the ringer of an old-fashioned cash register drifted to her ears and someone called out a friendly greeting to someone else—

she didn't have the heart to burst his bubble. It wouldn't hurt her to go along, and at least the next few days would be peaceful.

She sighed, then steered the cart toward the meat refrigerators. There were five turkeys left in the case. She started to take out the smallest one, but Charles came up behind her and picked up the largest one instead.

"Do you remember how to do a turkey?"

It was a natural enough question, for she usually had Christmas dinner catered. Yet Judith felt that he meant much more. Do you remember how to be my wife? Do you remember how to be happy? Do you remember how to love me?

She averted her eyes from his perceptive scrutiny. "I remember."

They shopped in relative harmony after that. Although their conversation was trivial—primarily concerned with which brand and how much to get— Judith recognized once again just how important her attitude was to relieving the strain between them. At least the overt strain. She had only to maintain that pleasant facade for the rest of the week. She'd done it for years. She could manage for a few more days.

She was just congratulating herself on her plan when she rounded a corner and spied Jennifer speaking with a stranger. The man was average height with an average build. Healthy looking, she might have thought under different circumstances. But he had long hair pulled back into a ponytail at his neck, and wore a fringed leather jacket. And he had no business talking to her little girl.

"Not only do they rot the teeth, but they rot the brain as well—"

"Jennifer." Judith interrupted the man and threw her arm protectively around her daughter's shoulders. "I was looking for you, dear," she said, sending Jennifer a cautionary look. "We're about to check out. Come along now. Excuse me," she added as she edged past the man. For a moment their glances met.

"It's all right, ma'am. I was just suggesting she buy dried fruits instead of those Twinkies. Just as sweet, but much better for her."

Judith hesitated. "Yes, well. Thank you." Then she looked down at Jennifer. "We really must be going, dear. Your father is waiting."

"Can I get the dried apricots *and* the Twinkies?"

"Fine." Judith gave the man one last parting glance. He was not as young as she would have expected, judging only by his long hair and eccentric dress. Probably near her own age, she realized. And his eyes did seem kind—serene, in fact. Not at all what she had feared when she'd first seen him with Jennifer. Still, he *was* a stranger, and Jennifer must learn to be more wary. She urged Jennifer past him.

"'Bye," he called. "Merry Christmas."

Jennifer turned back to him with a bright smile. "Merry Christmas."

"Merry Christmas," Judith added as well. But she kept one hand firmly on Jennifer's elbow.

"Don't you know better than to speak to strangers?" she whispered angrily once they were out of sight. "Haven't we told you that over and over again?"

"I was just being polite," Jennifer defended herself. "Always be polite to grown-ups. Isn't that what you say? Jeez, Mom. It's no big deal."

Judith didn't answer. It *had* been no big deal; she

knew that now. Jennifer could come to no harm in the grocery store with both her parents within earshot. Yet she'd felt so vulnerable when she'd seen that man with her daughter.

But it was more than that, she realized. The real truth was that she felt excruciatingly vulnerable to everything lately, and so she had overreacted.

As she gazed down into Jennifer's resentful young face, Judith sighed. "It's all right, dear. I guess I'm just a little touchy today. The trip and all," she added with a wan smile.

"Here's the rice," Charles said as he came up to them. "And canned mushrooms. There were no fresh ones." He added the items to the basket. "What kind of cereal does Alex like?"

"Honey Nut Cheerios. Or Shredded Wheat. What else do we need?"

"Don't forget candy canes," Jennifer suggested. "We have to have candy canes."

Charles rubbed the top of Jennifer's head affectionately. "We're going to have a great Christmas, Jenn. Just you wait and see."

"Dad!" the twelve-year-old complained, ducking away from his hand. She quickly combed her fingers through her hair to straighten where he'd mussed it.

But Charles's exuberance was not dimmed. "She'll see, won't she, Jude?"

Judith gave him her most determined smile. "I'm sure it will be lovely."

Outside in the car Alex was growing restless. How long did it take to buy a few groceries, anyway? He flicked off the pounding rhythms and piercing wail of

a Skid Row tape, then removed his headphones while
he rewound the tape.

A car pulled away from the parking space to the
right of the sedan. Beyond it he saw an old-time
hitching post and watering trough. Three kids were
clustered near the trough. The smallest one was poking at it with a stick, while the other two looked on.
Then the middle-sized one ran over to an old yellow
van and jumped up through the opened side door. In
a minute she was back with something in her hand—
he could see now she was a girl.

Alex watched as she and the older boy began to
play hacky-sack. He'd seen it done before, tossing a
small leather ball back and forth with the feet. The
older boy was pretty good, but the girl would miss
every now and again. Although the boy always
laughed at the girl's mistakes, she didn't seem to
take offense, for she would laugh also, then try again.

On a whim Alex decided to get out of the car. It was
probably as cold inside as it was outside, he decided,
so he might as well stretch his legs. Anyway, his dad
hadn't said he had to stay *in* the car. He shoved his
Walkman under the front seat, then opened the door,
climbed out, and stretched.

All around him the small parking lot was hemmed
in by towering pines and birch trees. Aside from the
occasional car passing on the highway and the laughter of the children by the van, it was amazingly quiet.
A good place to play music, he thought with a glim-
mer of interest. Then he remembered that he didn't
have his amp and his rising mood fell again.

Why did his father always have to spoil things?
Why did they always have to do what *he* wanted to

do? Go away to the stupid mountains. Leave his amplifier behind.

Miss the Metallica concert.

Angry once more, he hopped onto the trunk of the car, feet on the front bumper and not caring whether the studs on his jeans might mar the Mercedes's finish, as his father always claimed. Who cared about a stupid car anyway?

He scowled down at his hands, then turned to stare at those noisy kids. The little one was hitting the ice-covered water with a stick. He—or she, Alex couldn't tell, the way it was bundled up in an old brown hooded coat—gripped the stick with two hands and pressed the pointed end against the ice. In a moment the ice broke and the child's hands plunged into the water.

Stupid kid, Alex thought as he watched the child jump back, shaking water from the now-wet ends of the coat sleeves. When the child looked around, as if to see if anyone were watching, Alex realized it was a girl. When she caught him watching her, she grinned, then picked up the stick again. Once more she poked at the ice, but carefully, so as not to get wet again.

Alex looked away, but at a triumphant shout, his eyes veered back to the kids. The hacky-sack game had taken a different turn, it seemed, for it was the older boy who leaned down to pick up the leather toy.

"I got you that time!" his sister crowed. "What do you think of that, Robbie?"

The boy grinned and said something, but Alex couldn't make it out.

"Hi."

Alex twisted his head to find the littlest girl standing straight in front of him.

"Hi," Alex grunted. She was a little bitty thing, with messy curls around her face, and cheeks bright red from the cold. Her hands were red, too, he noticed. They must be freezing after getting wet.

"Wanna play with me?"

"No." He stared down at her. "You better go dry off or your fingers will freeze and fall off."

She stared at him skeptically but nonetheless glanced down at her hands. Once she was sure all her fingers were there she stuck one of her hands in her pocket. The other still clutched the stick.

"They won't fall off." She swung the stick aimlessly around her.

"Not now. But after you go to sleep tonight they might."

She stopped swinging the stick. She didn't seem so sure. "How do you know?"

Alex stifled his smile and forced himself to look grim. He leaned forward, bracing his elbows on his knees. Bending two of his fingers back, he held his left hand up. "That's how."

With a gasp she jumped back. Her eyes were as wide as saucers and her face lost some of its rosiness. Then she threw the stick away, turned, and ran toward the yellow van.

"Hey, watch it," Alex yelled when the stick hit the trunk next to him. He jumped down from the car, but as she barreled away, his irritation turned to chagrin. "Stupid kid," he muttered.

Across the lot the other two children stopped their game at the youngest one's sudden approach.

"My fingers!" Alex heard her cry. "They're gonna fall off!"

The boy knelt down before her and wrapped her in his arms. Alex couldn't make out their muffled conversation, but he saw all three of them turn to stare at him.

Stupid kid, he thought again. *Can't even take a joke.* He bent down nonchalantly and picked up a handful of gravel. Then he idly began to toss the chips at a towering birch tree that stood at the edge of the parking lot. The first three tosses missed. But the fourth hit, as did the fifth.

He chanced a quick glance at the three kids. The little girl was standing in the doorway of the van; her brother was helping her remove her coat, then her brightly colored sweater as well. The other girl came out of the van with dry clothes, and the child was swiftly bundled into them. For added measure she donned mittens and her brother wound a red-and-white striped muffler around her head and throat.

Alex threw another rock, but he was aware the moment the three children started toward him.

"Hey!" the boy named Robbie called out to Alex. But Alex only threw another rock. It hit the tree squarely and ricocheted back into the gravel lot.

"Hey, you. Why'd you scare Josie that way?"

Alex turned to face them. The boy was smaller than he by almost a full head. He was younger, too, but that didn't seem to deter him.

"Tell her it's not true," the boy insisted.

Alex's eyes flitted over the little group. They were an odd threesome, all dressed in jeans and tennis shoes, but with a strange assortment of jackets and sweaters. Almost like foreigners, he thought.

"You mean about this?" Alex raised his left hand up as he had before.

"You see? You see?" the little girl called Josie cried. She clung to her big brother's arm. "I told you! Now my fingers are gonna fall off too!" At that she began to cry.

"Josie!" The boy turned to her for a moment, then thrust her into his other sister's arms. Before Alex could react, Robbie grabbed his left arm and twisted it back to reveal his folded-down fingers.

"See! Look, Josie, I told you it wasn't true!"

Alex shoved him hard and the smaller boy stumbled back. "Keep your hands off me, shrimp. Or I'll rip *your* fingers off."

The two girls sprang back from the glowering Alex, and their brother kept his distance, too. But his face reflected no fear, only disdain. "Does it make you feel good, scaring little kids?"

"Is it my fault she's too stupid to take a joke?"

"She's not stupid! She's only five years old."

They were still glaring at each other when Jennifer burst through the door of the grocery store. She was down the steps before she sensed the hostility in the scene. Then she skidded to a halt. The silence continued until Judith and Charles came out with several bags in their arms.

"Alex! Come here and help your mother!" his father called to him.

For a long moment the boys' gazes remained locked. Then Alex gave him a smug smile. "Gotta go, shrimp." He glanced over at the two younger girls. "Ciao, babies." He wiggled his fingers at them, then with a laugh turned away.

"What was that all about?" his father demanded with a suspicious frown.

"Just wishing the locals a merry Christmas, Dad. Just spreading some Christmas cheer." His tone grew bitter. "Isn't that what we came up here for?"

With a sharp motion he hurled the last of his rocks at the birch, but this one went wide of the mark and landed in some shrubbery beyond. Then he took one of the bags from his mother and with careful indifference put it into the trunk his father had opened. He got into the car and slammed the door—just a little harder than necessary, but not enough to get his father started up again.

Jennifer bounced into the car, chattering as usual, begging for her first high heels. But aside from shoving her leg away from his side of the seat, he ignored her. A Metallica tape in his Walkman easily drowned out the other conversation in the car. As they pulled out of the gravel lot, however, he looked out at the kids from the yellow van.

The two older ones were playing hacky-sack again, but the littlest girl was just sitting in the open door of the van. Her legs were swinging back and forth; for several beats she was in time with the music pounding in Alex's headphones. Then she glanced up at the passing Mercedes and her legs slowed their rhythm.

She was a cute little thing, Alex thought for a brief moment. Then he deliberately turned away from her watching eyes and turned up the volume of his music. Too bad she was so stupid.

Chapter *Three*

A quarter mil if it's a penny, Charles thought when he pulled the car into the gravel driveway. Rogers was obviously doing very well at the bank if his mountain getaway house was any indication. It had probably only cost half that to build, he decided as he scanned the multilevel house with a knowledgeable eye. If he'd bought the lot low—and knowing Rogers, he had—the man would turn a pretty penny when he sold the place.

Maybe *he* should look into resort developments, Charles mused. It would give him reason to get away from the city.

"This is it?" Alex unfolded his gangly form from the

car. His tone made his disappointment clear. "We're in the middle of nowhere. I bet they don't even have cable. No," he continued after spying the two single wires that fed electricity and telephone service into the house. "No cable. No MTV."

"I suppose you've never heard of a dish," Jennifer said as she alighted.

Alex ignored his sister's superior tone and stared up at the roof. Then he began a circuit of the house.

Charles sighed. He didn't know whether to hope they had a satellite dish or not. With cable they'd never see Alex. Without cable Alex would do nothing but sulk and complain. He stared up at the modern chalet-style house with its wood shake siding and two towering chimneys, and suddenly felt defeated. Who was he kidding? A mere change of scenery wasn't going to alter anything between him and Judith. Even the bright smile she assumed when she stepped from the car seemed only to emphasize the futility of it all. Once more she was smiling in the face of adversity. Why hadn't he recognized that habit of hers before?

"It's absolutely beautiful," Judith exclaimed. She drew Jennifer to her and gave her an encouraging squeeze. "We're going to have a splendid Christmas this year."

But like the puffs of her breath, which hung in the air only a few seconds before disappearing in the icy wind, Charles feared her enthusiasm was just as fleeting. Still, he resolved to match her efforts.

"It's great. Great. And look, Jenn. We can take a hike down into those woods to get a Christmas tree."

Jennifer followed the line of his gaze. "I like flocked trees best." Then she ducked out of her mother's embrace. "Is it long distance to call Clarisse from here?"

Judith sighed and her smile faded. "Yes. But perhaps later I'll let you make one call. One *brief* call," she added.

Charles opened the trunk and began to unload their luggage. He leaned Alex's guitar case against the side of the car. Almost at once, Alex sprinted up.

"Don't put that on the ground!" The boy yanked the flat case away from the car; then, without further word, he stalked toward the double entry doors.

"No satellite dish," Charles surmised. He shot Judith a wry look, and for a moment their eyes clung in that old familiar way, sharing an instant of understanding that only parents could comprehend. Then she looked away.

"Maybe we can get him to play some Christmas carols."

"Fat chance," Charles grumbled.

The house was even more impressive inside than out. Soaring ceilings, starkly modern details, and several large contemporary prints contrasted perfectly with large overstuffed furniture and plush carpets. In lieu of potted plants, several tall austere clusters of dried, curling branches stood in plain white ceramic pots.

"Amanda Olivier," Charles remarked as he placed his wife's bags down in the marble-floored foyer. He'd recognize Amanda's signature decorating touch anywhere.

"It works better in an office environment than a home."

Charles glanced at his wife. "I thought you liked her work."

Judith shrugged as she started up the stairs. "It's all right. I guess I've just seen too much of it. Jenn,

Alex, bring your bags up to your rooms. I don't want your stuff cluttering up the place."

The two children followed their mother up the stairs. Jennifer had her pink suitcase and matching clothes bag in tow. Alex held his guitar as if it were priceless, while his army-green duffel bag thumped up the polished wood stairs behind him.

Charles raked his hand through his hair. Unexpectedly, a shiver of fear went through him, but desperation demanded that he hold it at bay. This week together *would* be good for them, he told himself. They would be forced to deal together and talk.

He accepted the blame for their alienation from one another, for he knew enough about management techniques to have recognized the signs long ago. But he'd ignored the problem until now. They each led separate lives. This week, however, he was going to change all that.

That is, he was going to try.

He started to follow them up the stairs, then stopped. He ought to call the office first and let Doug know they'd arrived. He could also check the answering machine at home. At the same time he'd find the thermostat and turn up the heat.

A half hour later it began to snow. The sun was hidden behind a heavy layer of low-hanging clouds. The wind had picked up, and beyond the driveway the pine trees swayed in the erratic gusts.

A white Christmas, Charles thought. Why did that idea, which should have been so appealing, suddenly just seem bleak?

"It's snowing," he said, standing before the large master bedroom window, his fists thrust into his pants pockets. Behind him he heard Judith hanging up the last of their clothes.

"I hope it's not so deep that you and Alex can't go out for a tree. Is there a hatchet here?"

"An ax. You need an ax to cut down a tree. Rogers said the house has everything we need."

He turned to face her then, and for the space of two heartbeats they stared at each other. His words seemed to linger in the chill air. *The house has everything we need.* Did it have the magic formula that would heal the wounds that lay between them? the ludicrous thought came. He'd brought them here with that hope, he realized. He wanted to recapture happiness—somehow reenter their past. Only this time he would do things differently.

But how? How?

He cleared his throat, but before he could speak, Judith began. "While I put the groceries away, why don't you see if you can find the Christmas decorations. I can make us dinner—how does a salad and lasagna sound?—while you build a fire."

Charles stared at his wife. In the soft yellowish light from the overhead lamp she seemed smaller than normal. And more fragile. She had aged lately—but then, so had he. Still, she remained a very beautiful woman.

Once more he cleared his throat. "We need to talk, Jude."

She seemed to shrink away from him. "Now? We've only just arrived. We're not even settled. Can't it wait until later?"

The ensuing silence was oppressive. Like a sharp physical pain, Charles's fear for their future tightened around his heart until he could hardly breathe.

"How much longer can we afford to wait?" he finally managed to say. "You can't raise the specter of —dammit!—of divorce, and not expect to talk about it. Christ!"

Judith swallowed. He saw the jerky movement of her throat and the suspicious glint of moisture in her eyes. But she didn't cry. "How appropriate. Profanity for Christmas," she replied in a brittle tone.

"What does that have to do with anything!" Charles exploded. "Our lives are falling apart and you're worried about my cursing? You're avoiding me, Jude. But it won't work."

"Really? Well, it worked for you for years. You're a master at avoiding what you don't want to see." She laughed, a harsh choking sound with no hint of mirth. "I learned from a master."

Charles was torn between wanting to shake her and wanting just to fold her into a desperate embrace. He trembled with the effort to do neither.

"I'm not avoiding anything now, Judith. I want to set things right between us. That's why I planned this trip. I want to begin again—"

"You want a lot, Charles. You always have. But you wanting it is not enough. It takes two to make a marriage work." She took a slow, shaky breath. "Did you never consider that I might *not* want it?"

If she had torn his heart out by the roots, he could not have hurt more. Charles was terrified even to take a breath: he was sure he would break apart. The worst fear of his life had been exposed, and like a helpless creature never before subject to the light, he writhed before it.

He stepped back—recoiled—as if he'd been struck a physical blow. Then, unable to cope with her complete dearth of feelings for him, he jerked about and fled.

Judith stood there in the spacious bedroom, still staring at the place where Charles had been. But she did not see the wide picture window, or the silent snow beginning to edge the woodlands with white tracery. Instead she saw the stricken expression on her husband's face and felt the same wrenching pain he'd felt.

When had she become so cruel?

She honestly didn't know.

There had been a time when Charles had meant everything to her. Her world had centered on him, and later, on him and their children. Now she seemed, even to herself, completely self-centered. She wanted what *she* wanted, and too bad for anyone else.

Yet even now she wished it could be how it used to be. She wanted to be madly in love with her husband, so that nothing else would matter. Only everything else *did* matter.

She shook her head in confusion, unable to decipher what she wanted anymore. She wanted to feel that old thrill when she saw Charles, the one that centered low in the pit of her stomach. And she wanted to know he felt the same thrill for her. Yet the truth was, like the emotional part of the marriage, the physical side had suffered, too. Charles turned to her in bed as often as ever, but more and more she tried to avoid him. She felt so apart from him emotionally that the closeness of lovemaking seemed somehow dishonest. Even when she longed for him, she felt compelled to push him away.

It was madness, and yet she could not prevent it.

She turned back automatically to the task of putting away their clothes. His hung on the right side of the double-loaded closet, hers on the left. She placed his other items in the three right-side drawers of the large dresser and hers in the other three. On one nightstand went the book she was reading, *Night Vision* by Deborah Nicholas. On the other went today's copy of *The Wall Street Journal*. Finally she placed the empty luggage in the rear of the closet. Only when everything was well put away and she couldn't put it off any longer did she finally descend the wide stairwell.

The house was strangely hushed. Jennifer was on the phone—no doubt already taking advantage of Judith's moment of weakness in approving one call. Alex was perched in a bay window playing the guitar. How quiet the instrument was when it was not plugged into an amplifier. She could hardly hear it. Still, he shouldn't have his feet up on the upholstered seat, she noted absently. But she simply did not have the energy for an argument with Alex right now.

Her eyes skimmed the room restlessly, but she was unable to focus on anything. How would she manage an entire week here?

With a fortifying breath she deliberately buried that cowardly thought. Her children deserved a good Christmas. Charles obviously was trying to give them one; she could do no less. Even if it were the last Christmas they would celebrate as a family, some good might come of it. By losing the perfect family image he cultivated so desperately, Charles might come to realize how important it was to look deeper than just the surface.

He might, but somehow Judith doubted it.

* * *

"We'll all have our assigned chores," Charles said, pushing his half-eaten plate of food away. He bent over the list that lay next to his unused dinner knife. Anything to avoid the flat expression in his wife's eyes.

"I'll keep the fires going. Alex will keep a path open to the car." He looked up at his silent son. "I'll help you clear the driveway." Then his gaze shifted to Jennifer. "You will be responsible for breakfasts and lunches. That includes washing dishes, too."

"But Dad! That's not fair!" Jennifer cried. "Alex gets to play in the snow but I get all the cruddy work."

"Everyone keeps their own rooms neat and their beds made," he went on, ignoring her outburst. "You'll do dinners, Jude. Now, have I forgotten anything? Oh, yes, we'll all decorate the Christmas tree. Together. And we'll all go out tomorrow to pick one out and chop it down." He looked around at his family, willing someone to break the awful silence.

"Can I be excused?" Alex muttered. He didn't wait for an answer but scraped the chair back, nearly toppling it as he stood up. Jennifer was quick to follow. The one grabbed his headphones, shoved a tape into his Walkman, and retreated to the window seat he'd claimed earlier as his own. The other made a beeline for the television, rapidly flipping channels until the theme song for *Beverly Hills, 90210* came on.

"Lower it, stupid!" Alex shouted.

"Turn up your tape, *stupid*," Jennifer retorted.

Charles suppressed an urge to send them both to their rooms. Instead he stood up and began stacking the dishes. "Let's wash them together, okay?" He glanced briefly at Judith, then back at the dishes. He was so scared that his hands were shaking, but his very fear drove him on. He would not let their marriage end, no matter what she said. Somehow he would relight that spark. Somehow he would make her remember all the reasons she had once loved him. Long ago before the children had been born they had washed dishes together every night. Although he didn't expect his gesture now to win her over completely, he at least hoped it would be a start.

If he could simply hold his emotions at bay he knew he could succeed. It was just like closing a deal with a reluctant seller. Bit by bit, point by point, as long as he was careful and thorough, and never gave up, he could make this sale. He'd retrieved enough deals from the brink of disaster to know it could be done. But only if he remained calm and in control of himself.

That would be the hardest part.

"Well," he prompted her with a determined smile. "Are you going to relegate me to dishpan hands all alone?"

When she met his gaze with a forced smile of her own, he didn't know whether to be relieved or let down. "Do you want to wash or dry?" she asked.

"Whatever you say." He bobbled a glass but quickly caught it in his grasp. "Maybe we can find a radio station playing Christmas carols."

The kitchen was sleek and efficient, with just enough natural wood to prevent it from appearing completely austere. The sink was a gleaming white three-bowl affair with the very latest in acrylic and stainless steel attachments. It wasn't designed for washing dishes by hand, for there was no provision for a dish drainer. Dishes were meant to go directly into the dishwasher. But Charles found an old-fashioned square dish drainer in one of the lower cabinets and perched it somewhat precariously over one of the round sink bowls. Two dish towels lay in the back of a drawer.

"I'll wash," Judith said, as she filled the sink.

"Do you want gloves?"

"No."

He watched as she placed dishes in the hot soapy water. Her hands were so graceful; they always had been. She'd placed her rings on the counter, and he decided that made her look younger. More innocent. Her nails were not polished either, he realized. That was unusual.

He leaned past her to reach the mini-entertainment center built into a wall cabinet. They both jumped as sound filled the room, but Charles quickly lowered it. He punched the scanning bar several times, leaping from some sports event to classical music to rap and then some preacher, before the radio honed in on seasonal music.

As the strains of "The Holly and the Ivy" filled the small kitchen, for the first time that day Charles felt himself begin to relax. The tune was so upbeat and joyous, even though this rendition had no words. Were there any words to this song?

"Does this song have any words to it?" Judith asked.

Charles laughed and took the first glass from her. "I was just wondering that myself. I know the melody, but I can't remember any words."

There was a short silence. She handed him another glass. "Do you think we could talk Alex into playing a few Christmas songs?" she asked in a noncommittal voice.

A sudden poignancy filled Charles's throat with emotion. "Remember the year Jennifer was born? We had Christmas Eve dinner with Doug and Cora. Cora was playing carols on that old piano she used to have." He slowly dried the plate she handed him. "Alex was just a little thing."

"He was three."

"Yeah. Three years old. Remember how he stood on the piano bench next to Cora, singing his little heart out?"

"On the first day of Christmas my two loves gave to me, a party in a pear tree." Judith sang the version Alex had so innocently entertained them with those many years ago.

"A party in a pear tree," Charles repeated. "I wonder if he remembers that." He reached for another plate and his hand touched Judith's wet fingers.

She released the plate and concentrated on the silverware. "That song has always been hard to remember—all those verses."

"Yeah."

The strains of "The Holly and the Ivy" were replaced by the smooth baritone of Bing Crosby. "Looks like we'll definitely have our white Christmas this year," Judith remarked.

"Yeah."

They worked in silence, finishing the silverware and the casserole dish. From relaxed to edgy, somehow they were back to where they'd been before, and Charles didn't know how it had happened. He fiddled with the dishcloth after the last dish was dried.

"Judith," he began abruptly. "I want this Christmas to be good for all of us. I think . . . I think that pretending to get along is not a good solution. We need to talk about why you're so unhappy. Why you're so unhappy with our marriage—and with me."

He was trembling inside by the time his words were finished. They had to be said and he needed her to respond. Yet he was petrified with fear at the prospect of her answer.

Judith reached for her rings. One by one she slipped them on. The art deco one of onyx and baguette diamonds. The pearl one. And finally her wedding band. Then she looked up at him.

"It's not you, Charles. Not really. It's me. I think that maybe I need a life of my own. One that doesn't just revolve around you and the kids."

"That sounds like pop psychology to me. Like something you read in some magazine in the grocery store line. You *have* a life of your own. You have the time and money to do any damn thing you want, Jude. Anything at all. I even offered to set you up in a business all your own, if that's what you wanted. I don't tie you down. The kids don't, either. Not anymore. Hell, you have more free time than any ten people I know!" He realized he was shouting when she took a step back from him.

"Of course. You're right. And I'm not complaining about that. You're a good provider, Charles. I've never denied that. That's why you shouldn't take this as a personal . . ." She trailed off, shaking her head and clasping her hands at her waist.

"There's no way to take it *but* personally. It's *me* you want to abandon. Me and my kids."

"I wouldn't be abandoning anybody," she retorted in a frustrated tone. "Despite all your words to the contrary, *you* don't need me. And I'll still be there for Alex and Jenny."

Charles stiffened. How could she be so blind? "I *do* need you," he choked out in barely more than a whisper. "How can you think I don't?"

Her eyes welled with tears, and Charles took a perverse pleasure in it. At least he'd provoked *some* emotion in her.

"Not the way you once did." She turned then and hurried away, leaving Charles alone in the spotless kitchen. More alone than he'd ever been before.

He folded the dish towel in his hands, then refolded it again. He did need her. As much as he ever had. In even more ways than he had twenty years ago. How could she think otherwise?

Yet she did think otherwise, and that scared him. Even worse, however, was the question that dangled unsaid between them.

He'd wanted to ask her if she needed him anymore, only he was too afraid the answer was no.

T he house was warm. The fire blazed. The central heat was going full force. Though the snow outside came down in a thick white blanket, and the wind at times howled around the corners and eaves of the house, the cold was kept at bay.

But inside his heart, Charles felt frozen. He was as cold as the whole wintry outdoors, numb and shivering. All he wanted was to retreat to the bedroom and crawl into the bed. Maybe then he'd get warm. Maybe then he could find solace in the blankness of sleep.

But Judith was upstairs in their bedroom and he was too afraid of another confrontation with her to risk going up there. Instead he scanned the meager offerings on the tall, narrow bookshelves and wondered if she would come downstairs again tonight.

"You've watched that dorky show for an hour. It's my turn now."

"Says who?" Jennifer challenged her older brother.

"Says me, you stupid wuss."

"You're the wuss—"

"Yeah, right. You're showing your ignorance, *wuss,* 'cause the only wuss around here is *you.* Always has been. Always will be."

"You're such a fool," Jennifer spat right back. "Now, give me that remote!"

"Come and get it, punk."

When Charles finally turned around to face his children, Alex was holding the remote control for the television up out of Jennifer's reach, taunting her with it. "Come and get it," he egged her on.

"Daaaad!" Jennifer cried, stretching that one syllable into three. "Make him stop!"

"She's been hogging the TV ever since we got here. It's *my* turn."

"For God's sake, can't you two ever cooperate? Here, give me that." He grabbed the remote control unit from Alex, then punched at the various buttons until the television flicked off.

Charles turned and glared at his two children. "There will be no more bickering. Do you understand me? No more." He took a frustrated breath, then made himself speak more calmly. "There's a bunch of games on that bottom shelf. Go get one and then sit at the table and play it. No!" He forestalled their protests before they could voice them. "I'm not giving you a choice in this. Now, go!" he thundered.

If Charles had felt the chill of his family situation before, the furious silence he received now was positively arctic. Like wooden puppets, Alex and Jennifer did as he had ordered, but resentment was clear in even the least of their movements. A cabinet was jerked open; a game box was snatched out, then slammed down on the table. Two chairs were yanked back. One teetered and nearly fell over, but Alex righted it with a kick, then flung himself down on the seat.

"C'mon, cheeseball. Let's start this stupid game." His words were directed at his sister, but his sullen gaze was focused on his father.

"This is all your fault, you butthead!" Jennifer's words were a low hiss, but her tone was no less vehement.

Charles whirled, ready to shout again. But the sight of his children—two miserably hunched figures, flanking a worn gameboard and scattered plastic pieces—suddenly left him defeated. What was the point? They hadn't been here three hours, and already Judith was avoiding him and the children hated him. How had he screwed up so badly?

Disheartened, Charles made his way back to the kitchen. A shiver coursed through him and he decided to make a cup of hot chocolate. Then he spied the wall phone and changed direction.

Eleven quick jabs of his finger, four short rings, and a familiar voice answered the phone.

"Doug! It's Charles. How did things go with Garrington?"

"Charles. I sure didn't expect to hear from you already."

"Yeah, well, it's pretty quiet around here. Makes me a little antsy."

"You gotta learn to relax, guy."

"Yeah, yeah. And I will. It'll just take a couple of days. So, did you get to Garrington?" Charles asked, settling himself on a chrome-and-leather kitchen stool.

"Actually, I found out he and his wife are going to the Odyssey Christmas Ball tonight. Cora had bought tickets, although we weren't going to attend. You're a lot better at that social stuff than I am. But we're going after all. Cora's friend Beverly—that's Richard Beasley's wife—she's going to introduce Cora to Garrington's wife while I hobnob with the man himself. So . . ."

"Sounds like you have it all under control."

"I'll know in a couple of hours. Look, I gotta go finish getting dressed. How about I call you in the morning?"

"Sure. Sure, that sounds fine. Good luck, guy."

"Hey, like you always say, you make your own luck with guts and perseverance."

"With balls and belligerence." Charles laughed.

When he hung up the phone he felt better. At least business was good. A muffled expletive brought him back to the moment.

"You're a dork!" Jennifer's shrill cry came. "I hate you!"

Before Alex's retort could come—before Charles could force himself to deal with his children again—the unexpected chime of the doorbell echoed through the house.

The doorbell? Charles glanced out the kitchen window to the thick snow striking silently against the triple-insulated glass. Who in their right mind would be out in such weather?

"Dad. Somebody's here."

"Don't open the door," Charles yelled as he hurried through the house. From the corner of his eye he saw Judith coming down the stairs, drawn by the still reverberating chime.

He flipped on the outside light, opened the sleek inlaid front door, and stopped before the double glass storm doors. Outside, huddled on the front landing with the wind and snow whipping at them, were a group of heavily bundled people. A family, Charles realized when he recognized a child in the tallest figure's arms. Two more children and a woman hugged one another for warmth behind the man.

"Oh, my goodness." Judith hurried up behind him and tried to open the doors.

"Wait a minute, Jude." Charles pulled her back.

"We can't leave them out there—"

"I know. I know. But you need a key for the storm doors. Here." He fished around in his pocket for the key ring Rogers had given him. In a moment he had the doors opened and the pitiful group stumbled into the small foyer.

"Come in. Come in," Judith said as Charles forced the doors closed against the bitter wind. It was a lot colder out there than he'd realized.

"Thank you," the man mumbled past his frost-encrusted mustache. "Thank you." He shuffled stiffly forward, out of the crowded entry alcove into the foyer. He still held the child tight, but one of his hands moved in a jerky fashion up the little one's back. The woman and the two older children seemed to be holding one another up; they were too frozen to do more than hobble forward.

For a moment there was complete silence. The newcomers huddled together, still coated with snow and edged with a hoary frost on their eyebrows and around their mufflers. The Montgomerys stood across the foyer from them just staring. A minute before they'd been embroiled in their own private turmoil. Now they were all at a loss.

"We were in an accident . . . Our van . . ." The man trailed off, as if even talking took too much energy.

Alex and Jennifer scrutinized their unexpected visitors with renewed curiosity. Charles was torn between natural feelings of caution, and irritation that a bunch of strangers had suddenly been forced upon them. What were they supposed to do with them anyway?

Judith, however, rose to the occasion. With a sharp click she closed the inner doors. "My lord, how did it happen? No, that can wait. Alex, you get blankets and sweaters—any dry clothes, socks. Anything. Jenn, make hot chocolate. Lots of it. Go!" she ordered when they hesitated. "Charles, turn the furnace up all the way, then come back and help me with these children."

"You want us to bring our clothes down here for them to wear? *Our* clothes?" Jennifer asked. On her face was an expression of incredulity, as if she could not believe her mother could actually expect such a thing of her. Charles couldn't help but silently agree with Jennifer.

"Yes, Jennifer." Judith gave her daughter a stern look. "You have enough for three people up there."

"Don't worry, Jenn. I'll be real careful in what I select." Alex smiled sarcastically.

"Don't you *dare* touch any of my clothes," Jennifer snapped. She shot her mother a pained look. "*I'll* do it."

"Please. You don't have to put yourselves out for us," the man interjected through teeth chattering from the cold. "I know we're disrupting you. We . . . we just need to get warm and . . . and call someone."

"You need to get out of those wet clothes," Judith contradicted. "We can dry your own clothes quick enough and give them back to you. Now get going," she ordered her two children. "You, too," she added with a glance at Charles.

Charles quickly raised the thermostat to eighty degrees. There was nothing to do but take these people in, he knew. They couldn't leave them outside in this weather with no other houses around for miles. But he didn't have to like it, he fumed as he returned to the living room.

Under Judith's direction the family had laid down their knapsacks and other clutched bundles. The man was fortyish, Charles saw, as was his wife. The three children—a boy around thirteen or fourteen, a girl a little younger than Jennifer, and another little girl, five or so—all appeared to be in a state of shock. They just stood there as Judith rushed around trying to make them more comfortable.

"Charles, come help me," she ordered.

He did as she instructed, though he didn't really want to. They helped remove wet shoes and socks from the children's frozen feet. They replaced their icy pants with warm thermal underwear and layered

on sweat shirts, sweaters, and blankets. The three
children didn't say a word. They only did as directed:
stuck out an arm or leg as necessary.

Jennifer and Alex stood to the side watching everything. For once they were both at a loss for words.
But Jennifer frowned when the middle girl was
folded into her pink-striped Laura Ashley robe.

The man and the woman helped each other as best
they could, but their movements were awkward and
interrupted by violent shivers.

"We hit an ice patch," the man said when he had
caught his breath enough to speak. "About a mile up
the road. I veered to avoid a rabbit. The van spun
. . . We would have gone over the edge, but a big old
oak caught us—"

"You're okay now," Judith murmured as she
pressed a mug of hot chocolate into his hands. "Can
you hold this?"

"Yeah. Yeah, I think so. Thanks," he added with a
shaky smile.

Charles had the youngest girl on his lap. He'd just
pulled one of Jennifer's sweaters over her head when
she started to struggle away from him.

"Mama!"

"Hold on, hold on," he muttered. "Just wait while I
get these socks on you. Jennifer, don't just stand
there. Help me."

"Me? What am I supposed to do?"

"Josie, hush, sweetie. I'm here."

The woman fell clumsily to her knees before
Charles and put her arms around the little girl, rock-
ing her in the ageless way parents have always
rocked their children. With that movement she
seemed to release all the emotions the entire family

had been holding back. The little girl, Josie, began to cry. Her mother began to cry. The two older children —now dressed in a motley collection of Alex and Jennifer's clothes—burrowed weeping into their father's arms, and for a long moment there was no talking.

Charles looked helplessly up to Judith to see tears welling in her eyes. Alex and Jennifer had moved instinctively to her and she clasped them almost desperately to her.

At once Charles's frustration fled, to be replaced by far more complex emotions. It did not matter that Jennifer matched her mother's height, he realized, or that Alex topped her by five inches. They were both her babies and always would be. They needed her as much as he did.

That quickly, his heart seemed to catch in his chest. He wanted to go to them—to hold them so close they could never slip away from him. But young Josie still sat on his lap, and the woman crouched at his feet, holding her. He could only stare at his own little family, choked by the most powerful emotions he'd ever known.

God, but he loved them!

Finally the woman lifted her face from her daughter's curly head. "Thank you for taking us in. We . . . we couldn't have gone on much further."

Charles took the hand she offered. It was still icy cold, and he squeezed it tight, trying to impart some of his own warmth to her. It was true, they wouldn't have been able to go much farther. And in this storm . . .

How precious life was. How fragile. It could just as easily have been *his* family stranded in a blizzard this way. Once more emotions caught in his throat. "You're safe now," he managed to say. "You're all safe."

Their eyes met and held. Then she smiled and nodded. It took an effort for her to get to her feet. But she was able to lift little Josie in her arms and cross to stand beside her husband.

"You've saved us," the man said in a low tone. He looked down at his two older children as he struggled to control his voice. "I'm sorry we've barged in like this, but we didn't know what else to do. We couldn't get the van back on the road . . ." He shook his head, but he went on. "I'm Joe Walker. This is my wife, Marilyn, and our children—Robbie, Lucy, and Josie. I—" He broke off and had to compose himself. "I don't know how we can ever thank you."

Judith met Charles's eyes and for a moment they were connected, both sharing the same feelings of thankfulness for their own safety and that of their children. Then Judith cleared her throat. "Don't think anything of it. Anyone would do as much. I think, though, that we ought to get your children into bed. You, too," she added, for their exhaustion was plain. "Drink your chocolate and then we'll get you all settled. There's an extra bedroom with a double bed. Robbie can sleep in Alex's room. Lucy can sleep with Jennifer."

"Mother!" Jennifer objected in a low hiss. Alex, too, stared at his mother in disbelief. But Charles silenced them with a sharp look.

He stood up. "We didn't introduce ourselves. "I'm Charles Montgomery. My wife, Judith, and our children, Alex and Jennifer." He shook hands with Joe while Judith refilled their mugs. "Tomorrow we'll see about your car. Meanwhile, you should do as my wife said and all go to bed. You've been through an ordeal. Is there anyone you want to call to tell them you're safe?"

While Judith and the children carried the Walkers' meager possessions upstairs and settled Marilyn and her children in their beds, Charles showed Joe to the phone. For some reason the man looked vaguely familiar, but Charles couldn't figure out why. When Joe turned to the phone, however, Charles remembered. There was a ponytail tucked down in the man's thermal shirt. He had been at that grocery store—he and his kids from the yellow van. A worried frown creased Charles's brow, then deepened when Joe turned to him.

"The phone lines must be down."

Charles took the phone receiver from him. There was no dial tone. If the phone lines were out and the roads impassable, then they were all trapped together. Suddenly the reality of having a strange family forced upon them caught up with Charles. A pair of aging hippies and their raggedy children interfering with their Christmas. Was there anything else that could go wrong with this trip?

Charles watched Joe Walker trudge up the stairs. Only when the man turned into the hall and disappeared from view did Charles sigh and thrust one hand through his own close-cropped hair. Then he returned to the living room.

The silence in the spacious room seemed unnatural. Alex and Jennifer had settled down on either side of the game they'd abandoned earlier. Judith sat in a

large chair she'd pulled nearer the fireplace. Her feet
were tucked beneath her, and her hair was mussed.
She was staring pensively, not at the dancing flames,
but at their children. When he entered, however, everyone looked up.

"Well." He sighed once more as he seated himself
on the raised hearth and looked over at Judith.
"Looks like our guests may be here for a while. The
phones are already down and the way it's snowing,
the roads may be closed until the snowplows can get
out."

"What would have happened to them if we hadn't
been here?" Jennifer asked in a subdued voice. She
didn't sound like herself, and Charles knew she must
have had time now to consider the seriousness of the
Walkers' mishap.

He glanced uncomfortably at Judith. "It's silly to
worry about what might have been, honey. The fact
is, we *were* here." But he could tell Jennifer was not
reassured.

Judith shifted, then rose from the chair. She
crossed to Jennifer and leaned down to put her arms
around her. "They would have broken a window or
something and gotten inside. They would have been
okay."

"They were at that grocery store," Alex put in.
"While you guys were inside, I saw those kids in the
parking lot."

"That man talked to me inside, Mom. He's the one
who told me I should get the dried fruits."

"Yes. I remember." Judith looked at Charles. "He
seemed like a nice enough man."

"Yes, well, I'm sure we have nothing to worry
about," Charles agreed, rubbing his chin restlessly.

stairs, unaware how much his exit mirrored Joe Walker's earlier one. Holding a family together—*trying* to hold a family together—was the hardest work he'd ever done.

Chapter Five

T he house was as cold as the outdoors. One by one as they awoke, children and adults alike made their way downstairs to the huge fire that already blazed in the living room.

They were a haphazard-looking group, Charles decided, with blankets draped around nightgowns and terry cloth robes, and coats on top of pajamas and slippers. The only ones among them who appeared alert and fully awake were Joe and Marilyn Walker. While he brought in an armful of wood from the back porch and stacked it to the side of the hearth, she poured mugs of hot chocolate for the children, and hot coffee for the adults.

"Damn. What happened to the heat?" Charles asked.

Joe stood up and dusted off his arms, then looked at Charles. "The phones are still out, and now the electricity is, too. No lights. No radio or television. And no heat."

"What about the furnace?" Charles asked, trying to wipe the sleep from his eyes with icy fingers.

"The place is all electric. A lot of these weekend places are that way. It's easier than coal or oil, and cleaner. The only time it creates a problem is in storms like this. You might want to consider another form of heat for this place," he suggested.

"It's not my place," Charles responded irritably. "What's the matter with these weathermen? None of them said anything about a storm when we left yesterday." He watched as little Josie wormed her way inside the front opening of her father's coat, then was lifted into his arms and nearly lost inside the thick army-green wool.

"Take this coffee," Marilyn murmured. "I hope you like it with milk and sugar."

"My mother always gave us milk coffee like this," Judith replied over the edge of her steaming mug. She smiled at Marilyn, then let her gaze sweep over the others and come to rest on Charles. For a moment he was warmed by the old familiar glow in her eyes. But then she looked away and spoke once more to Marilyn.

"I think we need to get everyone properly dressed and get some breakfast going. I guess we'll all have to stay in the living room near the fire."

"We can use blankets to block off the stairwell so no heat escapes upstairs," Joe said. "The boys can bring down rugs and blankets so we can all be comfortable in here. If that's okay," he added, glancing at Charles.

Charles sighed and rubbed his brow. "Whatever. Do we have any battery-powered radios here? Alex, where's that Walkman of yours?"

"It's upstairs. But"—he glanced around sheepishly —"I fell asleep with it on last night, and I think the batteries are dead."

"Great! For once that damned thing could've helped, and you're telling me it's useless."

Judith edged nearer Alex. "There's a radio in the car."

Charles straightened. "A radio *and* a phone. Good thinking, Jude. I'll go out and try it."

"It's still snowing pretty hard. Be careful."

He smiled reassuringly at her. "Don't worry. With any luck I'll reach the state police and we'll have snowplows out here in no time."

While Charles prepared for his trek to the car, Judith and Marilyn got the house organized. "Get these potted sculptures out of here," Judith told Alex and Robbie. "Also, this hall tree. Bring in the dining table and chairs. And the rug, too. Put them over there."

"Here are candles and two antique oil lamps. I hope they work," Marilyn said as Josie came bounding down the stairs ahead of her father. He carried a wicker basket in his arms.

"The rabbit needs qui: and a warm spot."

Behind him Jennifer and Lucy came, loaded down with pillows. "We thought we'd scatter these pillows on the floor in front of the fire," Lucy said. "Like in Moonbeam's tepee."

"Moonbeam's tepee?" Alex gave the girl a skeptical look. "You know some Indians?"

Lucy shrugged. "I guess she's an Indian. Isn't she, Mom?"

Marilyn smiled, then peered a little cautiously at Judith. "My stepsister lives in a tepee part of the year. She's got a little Huron blood."

"She chews deerskins to make them soft," Robbie announced. He stared challengingly at Alex and Jennifer. "She says if you kill animals you should honor them by using every part of them. The skin. The bones. The meat—even the heart and the brains."

"That's disgusting!" Jennifer exclaimed.

"You like hamburgers, don't you?" he pressed on. "And leather shoes. Is that gross?"

"That's enough, Robbie." Marilyn gave him a warning gaze and he squelched whatever else he intended to say.

"Aunt Moonbeam is really nice," Lucy told Jennifer with a reassuring smile. She tossed her dark, waist-length hair behind her shoulder. "You'd like her. She makes the best bread."

"Acorn bread," Robbie said. "Acorn bread with wild honey. She smokes the hives and steals the honey."

"You can't make bread out of acorns." Jennifer glared at the laughing Robbie.

"Acorn bread," he continued. "Cattail pancakes. Daylily fritters."

"Robbie."

He glanced at his mother, then shot Jennifer a last look as he started toward the door. "They're all delicious. You should try them someday."

"Your brother is weird," Jennifer muttered to Lucy once he was gone.

"They *are* delicious." The younger girl defended her absent brother. "At least the way Moonbeam makes them they are."

Judith pushed the overstuffed couch nearer the fireplace and positioned two easy chairs next to it, smiling to herself as she did so. Jennifer and her crowd of well-dressed preteen princesses were as far removed from the likes of the Moonbeams of the world as it was possible to be. The Esprit-Gitano crowd was hardly likely to comprehend chewing deerskins and making acorn bread. Jennifer's reaction— disbelief and disgust—was not surprising. The truth was, Judith felt nearly the same. Still, it would be interesting to see how Jennifer and Alex got along with these children whose upbringing was obviously so unlike their own. Hopefully they would manage all right.

Judith watched Alex and Robbie turtle-walk into the big living room with the dining table suspended between them. Judging only by their looks, the two shaggy-haired boys appeared cut from the same mold. Both were skinny and dark haired, although Alex was a couple of years older and almost a head taller.

"Where are you from?" she asked Marilyn as they both unrolled the thick rug Joe had brought down from one of the bedrooms.

"We live near Edgard, but we'd been down at Reed City. There's a big crafts fair there every year right before Christmas. It's the last bazaar we attend before the winter lull."

"You sell things at fairs and bazaars?"

The slightly younger woman pushed her heavy dark hair behind her ear. "I'm a weaver. Joe is a wood craftsman and painter. We follow the fairs and festivals," she added with a faint edge of challenge in her voice.

"Oh." Judith combed the fringed edges of the oriental carpet with her fingers. The movie *Carny* was the first image that came to her mind, but she could not see this family in so seedy an environment. There was an unexpected wholesomeness about them. And even though following crafts fairs was a very odd existence, one completely unlike her own, a part of Judith understood its appeal. These people had done what every child dreamed of doing: they'd run away with the circus, more or less.

"Do you always bring the children with you?" she asked, truly interested. She sensed the slow relaxation of Marilyn's tension.

"Always. We're a family. We stick together. I was a teacher before I turned to weaving, so when we're on the road, I home teach. Once we get home I'll probably make them write their own versions of this latest of our adventures." She smiled. "It's always enlightening to see the same event from three very different viewpoints."

"Surely Josie is too young to write."

"She draws pictures, then tells me what captions to write for them. But it won't be long before she's writing them herself."

At that moment a cold rush of air announced Charles's return.

"Damn, but it's frigid out there!" He crossed to the fireplace slapping his hands against his arms while he backed as near the roaring flames as he dared.

Marilyn had a fresh mug of coffee for him before he

could ask for one. "Were you able to reach anyone on your car telephone?"

"No." A last violent shiver shook him. He removed his gloves with stiff fingers, and gratefully took the mug she offered. "I don't know if the weather has gotten to the cellular system itself—you know, knocking out the nearest tower. Or it could just be the car battery."

"Was the radio out, too?" Judith asked.

"Yeah. We're completely cut off." Judith met her husband's eyes, and the worry she saw there upset her more than anything else. They could manage without electricity so long as firewood was plentiful. They had shelter. They had food. She'd considered this an inconvenience—a rather large one, but still just an inconvenience. But Charles's worry fed her own and she suddenly recognized the seriousness of their predicament. They could be trapped here for days—for weeks even. There were no other homes for miles. That was one reason Charles had insisted they come here in the first place. No distractions.

But now it meant no help.

Her panic must have shown on her face, because Marilyn put a comforting hand on her arm and pulled her to sit on the couch. "Here, sit next to your husband and warm him up," she instructed as she pushed Charles down as well. "Everything's going to be fine. You'll see."

While she was there, smiling at them both in such a warm, motherly fashion, Judith believed her. But when Marilyn turned away to show Alex and Robbie where the mattresses were to go, fear washed over Judith again. Then Charles's arm came around her shoulder and pulled her close, and a whole new confusion swept through her.

"You're warm," he said. She felt him shiver and tuck her even nearer. "I've never been so cold as I was out there. The snow was already hip high in some areas. You could hardly see the car. And the wind—" He shook his head, then turned his face and kissed her left temple. "The wind slices right through you as if you don't have on so many clothes you can hardly move. I tell you, Jude, this is a bad storm."

"Do you think anyone will come for us?" she asked as his body warmth began to meet her own.

"No. Nobody in their right minds will go out in this blizzard. But it can't last forever." He sighed, then lowered his voice to a whisper. "It can't last forever, but it'll probably feel like forever, being stuck here with a bunch of strangers. 'Course, I guess it could be worse." He kissed her temple again, and this time she could feel his tight muscles relaxing. "I guess we're getting more of a white Christmas than we bargained for."

There was something reassuring about sitting in a deep couch with her husband's arm around her, and Judith let herself succumb to the feeling. Charles was not a bad husband. Not really. His intentions were good, and he really did love his family.

So how was it that she was so seriously considering leaving him?

That eternal debate between her head and heart was interrupted by the tearful appearance of the Walkers' youngest child, Josie.

"Mama!" She barreled headlong into her mother's arms. All that Judith could see of her was a riot of golden curls. The rest was hidden by her maroon-

and-blue sweater and her mother's surprised embrace.

"Josie. What is it? Oh, lord." Marilyn pressed a hand to her daughter's head, then looked at Judith. "She has a fever."

Judith was up at once. While she searched the medicine cabinets for a Tylenol, Charles fixed a pallet on a chair near the fireplace. When Joe came in with more wood and spied Josie in Marilyn's arms, he disposed of his load and crossed to kneel before the two.

"What's this, pumpkin?" He grinned at his daughter as he felt her flushed brow. "You can't get sick on us now. You'll miss out on all the fun."

"What fun, Daddy?"

"Well, we've got to go out and cut down a Christmas tree. And then decorate it." He sat on the couch and eased Josie into his arms. "Plus, I thought we'd play charades tonight. Like we always do around the campfire. I know how much you like charades."

The five-year-old settled into his embrace. "But this isn't a campfire."

"Oh, yes it is. It's an inside campfire. We're camping out inside 'cause it's too cold to sleep in a tent."

"Can she swallow a tablet? Or should I dissolve it in something?" Judith asked.

"I'm *not* a baby." Josie sat up and took her medicine. Everyone had come into the living room and her eyes swept the group. When her gaze touched on Alex, however, her baby face became fearful. She looked back up at her father. "Will my hands fall off? Will they?"

"What? Where did you get such a silly idea, sugar? Your hands aren't going anywhere. You're going to be fine. Just fine."

"But he said—"

"You see what you've done?"

Everyone's eyes turned to Robbie, then followed his angry glare to Alex.

"Hey, I was only joking."

"She's only a little kid. You can't joke with her the same way you do with your sister."

"Alex, what is this all about?" Charles demanded.

A slow flush crept up Alex's face and he shifted uncomfortably from one foot to the other. "It was just a joke. She got her hands wet yesterday. At that store. And I told her . . . I told her she better dry them or her fingers . . . well, I told her they might fall off. But I was just joking," he finished defensively.

"*His* fingers fell off," Josie told her father. "Make him show you."

"Alex," Judith said, embarrassed by the whole situation. "Show her you were joking."

Alex raised his hands and wiggled his fingers. "I was joking," he repeated, scowling at the child. Then he jerked around and stalked out of the room.

There was an awkward silence. Judith wanted to run after Alex, yet that seemed inappropriate. Jennifer edged next to her, and she put an arm around her daughter's shoulder instead. Only when Lucy crossed to Josie did the atmosphere change.

"Look, Josie. I know an even better trick than Alex did. See?" She held her two hands up together, then folded one thumb back while circling it with a forefinger. "See?" She pulled her hands apart so that it appeared she had pulled off the end of one of her thumbs. "Look, I'll show you how to do it too."

Under her playful instructions, Josie began to

smile. When the little girl had perfected the hand trick, she laughed out loud. "I'm going to trick Alex. Don't let anybody tell him. Let *me* fool *him* this time."

"Okay, pumpkin. But right now you need to rest." Joe carried her to the bed fixed for her in one of the overstuffed chairs. "Close your eyes and take a nap."

The child yawned as he tucked a comforter around her. "Will you sing me a song?"

"Sure, pumpkin." He sat down on the rug in front of her and began to rub her feet.

As he began to sing a slow Christmas song, Judith found herself sliding her hand up and down Jennifer's arm in sync with the melody. His voice was deep and rich and the familiar carol was mesmerizing. Calming. Jennifer glanced up at her mother with a small smile on her face. When Lucy sat down beside her father, however, Jennifer ducked out of her mother's embrace and knelt down beside the little group.

"Where's Roger Rabbit?" Josie murmured. "Is he okay? Did you feed him, Lucy?"

"Not yet, but I will."

"Let me. Let me." Jennifer jumped up. "I'll get him something really good to eat, Josie. Then I'll move his box right next to you."

As Jennifer departed for the ice-cold kitchen, Judith noticed Charles standing before the fire. He had one foot propped up on the wide brick hearth. His hair was sticking up in all sorts of directions. His sweater was buttoned crookedly and his shirt collar was bunched up. Most uncharacteristic, she thought. But then, so was the troubled expression on his face.

She was accustomed to his "trouble at the office" expression. It generally had an edge of anger to it, and of determination. His "trouble at home" expression was generally more frustrated. But his face now seemed more that of a lost little boy's. She started to go to him, but before she could, he scowled.

"Damn car phone!" He looked over at her. "I should have gotten a newer model a long time ago. And a better car battery. We wouldn't be cut off like this now. That's the first thing I'm going to do when we get home. Get a new car phone and battery."

Judith stared at him. "This storm probably has construction stopped everywhere. There can't be anything going on at the office. Try to relax," she added, mindful that Joe and Marilyn could overhear them.

"Just because a job site is shut down, it doesn't mean other even more important business can't progress. You should know that. It's not the mall project in Badington I'm worried about. It's Greenmont Center. The demolition permits. That damned wishy-washy Garrington and his busybody of a wife." He slapped the mantel hard, then sighed. "And now we're cooped up here—our whole Christmas shot to hell."

"At least if Alex and Jennifer are asked to write a paper on 'how I spent my Christmas' it'll be more than a litany of the gifts they received."

Charles scowled at her. "Since when have you liked roughing it?"

Judith shrugged. "I didn't say I liked this situation. I only meant that we have to make the best of it. Find some good in it." She smiled. "You're the one who always says nothing is ever a complete loss. Does that apply only to business?"

He stared at her a long moment. "I guess the day will come when we laugh and reminisce about this—

'remember that Christmas?' Sort of like reminiscing about the old days before the business took off. When we struggled for every dime. Looking back, it doesn't seem nearly as rough as it was."

Judith's smile faded. "No, it doesn't seem like it was rough at all."

Just then a shout erupted from the kitchen. Jennifer and Alex.

Judith hurried toward the angry cries, glancing guiltily at the Walkers as she did. Marilyn and Robbie were stacking the firewood while Joe resumed singing to prevent Josie from awakening. Only Lucy looked up. Beneath the child's thick straight bangs, her eyes were amazingly clear and disturbingly perceptive. Like a tiny wise woman, Judith thought as she dashed into the kitchen. There was no time to elaborate on that, however, for she had her own two children to deal with.

"What in heaven's name is going on?"

Alex and Jennifer both stood before the opened refrigerator. One held a head of lettuce, while the other held a plastic bag of carrots. They were glowering at each other, and not even Alex's superior height and strength could intimidate Jennifer.

"I'm feeding Roger Rabbit, but this heavy-metal lame-brain is being a jerk. As usual," she added in a venomous tone.

"Roger Rabbit," Alex scoffed. "He's a real rabbit, not a cartoon character, like you."

"Stop it!"

Judith jumped at Charles's thunderous words. He had come up behind her, and now he surveyed his family furiously.

"Haven't you two got anything better to do than

fight every single minute of the day? Can't you go even a little while without jumping down each other's throats?"

"We could watch TV," Alex answered bitterly. "But the stupid electricity is out. We could listen to the radio—oops, I forgot. No electricity."

"Alex," Judith warned. But in youthful outrage he plunged recklessly on.

"I know." He gave his sister an exaggerated smile. "Let's play Monopoly—no, Chinese checkers—no. How about tiddlywinks!"

Charles shouldered past Judith. In the icy kitchen everyone's breath hung in the air. Frigid puffs of anger, colder even than the storm outside.

"Go to your room!" Charles yelled when he was face-to-face with Alex. "And don't you dare come down here till I say you can!"

Alex looked ready to yell back at his father, but Judith grabbed his arm. She frowned at Charles.

"It's too cold upstairs. There's no heat."

"Good! Maybe he'll cool off!"

"Charles, you're being unreasonable."

"Me! Me? Dammit to hell, Jude! I'm the only one in this family who *is* reasonable. I've given him everything any kid could ever want. Yet all I get back is complaints, sarcasm, and a frown. All he *ever* does is frown. And Jennifer—if it weren't for her always asking me for money, she'd never even notice me. Then there's you. I built you a mansion. You can buy whatever you want from any store in New York. In the world! But are you satisfied? No. No, you repay me by threatening me with divorce—"

He stopped abruptly.

Alex and Jennifer were staring at him in horror.

Judith knew she should deny what he'd said. Yet she couldn't muster the words. When the children's eyes swung to her, she could do no more than weakly shake her head.

Into that terrible silence Joe Walker's voice was a welcome relief. "Jennifer, have you got the rabbit's breakfast? And Alex, I need help cutting more firewood. You, Robbie, and I can take turns with the ax."

The children obliged him at once, fleeing silently from the kitchen. Then he turned his perceptive gaze on Judith and Charles. "The acorn doesn't fall too far from the tree. You can't expect your children to exhibit an inner peace when neither of you do."

The quiet words struck Judith's heart with painful accuracy. Even Charles was temporarily silenced. Then Joe left and Charles's temper returned.

"Who the hell does he think he is? He's got a hell of a nerve barging into our lives—ruining our Christmas—and then preaching to us!"

"He didn't barge in here, at least not by choice. And they aren't ruining our Christmas," Judith said, unable to still the tremble in her voice. "They're just a nice family, a pair of artists who had the misfortune to get stuck here with us. The truth is, we couldn't manage a happy Christmas under the best of circumstances. We'll probably ruin *their* Christmas." She smiled bitterly. "The acorns haven't fallen too far from the tree, have they? Alex and Jennifer—" She broke off. Joe's words seemed to echo in her ears. "Are you peaceful inside, Charles? I know I'm not. So how can we expect it of them?"

"You've always been too easy on them."

"And you've always avoided what you don't want to see. The problem is us, not them. They're just the symptom, like a stomachache that won't go away. Pepto-Bismal may mask the pain for a while, but the ulcer's still there, Charles. It's still there."

He shoved his hands into the pockets of his coat. "More pop psychology? The fact is, everyone in this family just needs to try a little harder. I can't do it all by myself."

"All by yourself?" Judith laughed, but she felt more like crying. "You haven't got a clue, have you? Well, pay attention to this, Charles Montgomery. You don't know what 'all by myself' really means. But you will soon. You will soon."

Chapter Six

Charles stayed in the kitchen. If he hadn't known otherwise, he would have thought he was having a heart attack, so acute was the pain that gripped his chest. But he'd been given a clean bill of health only a month ago. His doctor had said he was just working too hard. His stomach pains, constant weariness, and occasional chest pains were stress related. Take a vacation, the doctor had advised, and all those symptoms would go away.

But Charles's stresses were not due to work. And this vacation was making it painfully clear.

Out of habit he crossed to the wall phone and lifted the receiver to his ear. Nothing. Not a sound. His fingers caressed the length of the receiver for a moment, and then he slowly placed it back in its holder.

Footsteps hurried up the stairs. He heard Judith's voice and then Marilyn's. Lucy laughed out loud and Jennifer began to giggle. Then Joe Walker called for Robbie and Alex, and in a moment footsteps clattered down the stairs. The three came through the kitchen and Charles immediately straightened his posture. His hands tightened on the kitchen counter when Alex went by without glancing up at all. Robbie followed, shooting Charles a quick curious glance as he hurried past.

Joe hesitated when the two boys went outside. But Charles's rigid posture must have warned him away. With a sigh the man pulled a knit hat down over his ears and joined the boys.

Charles couldn't help himself. He rubbed a clear spot on the kitchen window to watch them. Joe had an ax. He'd probably found it in the basement. Now he had both boys out by a chopping block. Charles had a hard time imagining the banker, Rogers, cutting firewood. But Joe Walker—he fit the image, and though it should not have, that realization bothered Charles.

There had been a time when he had fit that image, too, Charles recalled, back when he'd been a young man visiting his grandparents. He'd cut more than his share of wood way back then. But Alex didn't know that. Charles had never even thought about teaching Alex how to chop wood. They purchased it by the cord for the fireplaces at home.

His brow creased as he realized that Alex probably saw him only as a businessman. Someone like Rogers, who didn't appear able to build a fire, let alone cut the fuel for it.

He watched in increasing despair as Joe had the boys haul several unsplit logs nearer. Even through the driving snow, Charles could see the interest on Alex's face as the man gestured and explained. Then with just a few well-aimed blows, Joe split the log.

Alex gathered up the pieces while Joe positioned another log. Robbie took the ax then, and went to work. Although it took him several more swings, he, too, quickly reduced the heavy log to more manageable fuel for the fireplace. Robbie did another, and then another, but Charles didn't watch the youngster work. His eyes were trained on Alex, who was standing off to the side with Joe.

The man had his hand on Alex's shoulder as he spoke to him. He said something and Alex laughed. A full, unrestrained grin lifted the boy's face, and once more Charles felt an ache in the vicinity of his heart. Why couldn't he bring that kind of expression to Alex's face? Maybe if they played some tennis . . .

Finally it was Alex's turn. Joe showed him how to hold the ax: left hand near the curved end, right hand free to slide with the stroke. He showed Alex how to judge the correct distance he should be from the log, and how to position his feet. Then he and Robbie stood back to the side.

Snow swirled against the window. It coated the three figures outside and gave the scene a Christmas-card quality. Alex looked over at Joe and said something that caused him and Robbie both to laugh. Charles wished he knew what it was.

He watched with tensed posture as Alex lifted the heavy ax and then swung. Too tentative, he thought, as the metal head glanced off the log, only toppling it over. Joe and Robbie both came forward with advice and gestures. Alex nodded, then righted the log. His brow was creased in concentration as he focused on the log. Once more he swung, and this time the ax bit deep into the seasoned oak.

He mimicked Joe's and Robbie's earlier actions to knock the log free, then positioned it again. In all it took him almost twice as many swings to split the log as it had taken Robbie, and he was blowing hard when he finished. But the expression on his face was exultant.

Joe clapped him on the back and Robbie handed him a wood chip from among the pieces scattered in the snow. Alex grinned and slipped it in his pocket. Joe took the ax and split several more logs before handing it on to Robbie. They continued on that way, the three of them taking turns with the work while the stack of fuel grew and grew.

They talked as they worked, and though their cheeks and noses grew ruddy with the cold, they clearly were warmed by their activity. Charles, by contrast, grew colder and colder. He shivered in the frigid kitchen and his teeth chattered, but still he could not tear himself away from the window. Only when he saw them lay the ax aside and begin to gather up the wood did he step away. Before the trio could reenter the kitchen, he retreated to the living room.

He noticed at once that the chaos in the room had disappeared. Though the room was a far cry from the contemporary sleekness its designer had originally intended, its new coziness was actually more appealing. Rugs covered the gleaming wood floors almost entirely. The upholstered furniture was clustered tightly before the fire, with a low coffee table in the middle. Quilts and comforters from the bedrooms were folded over the backs of the couches and chairs so that anyone could easily snuggle up for warmth. The dinner table and chairs took up the corner near the now curtained-off dining room.

Though it was still not toasty warm in the big room, the fire Joe had built earlier had settled down and now was exuding a steady, glowing heat. Josie was curled up in one of the big chairs, fast asleep with her thumb in her mouth. Judith sat in the chair next to her. Although her eyes were closed, Charles was certain she was not asleep.

Jennifer and the other girl were sitting cross-legged before the fire. The Monopoly board was set up on the coffee table. Paper money, dice, and yellow and orange cards were spread out, forgotten for the moment as they both leaned over to look into the rabbit's box.

"Leave the poor animal to rest," Marilyn mildly rebuked the two as she bent forward, potholder in hand. She fiddled with several cast-iron rods attached to one side of the massive fireplace and finally managed to make them swing forward past the main heat of the fire. She looked up with a pleased expression on her face. When she saw Charles watching her she smiled.

"Whoever built this house did us an enormous favor by including these swivel pot hangers in their new fireplace."

"I'm sure it was done for its picturesque quality, not for any real cooking," he replied.

"Well, picturesque they may be, but they're practical, too. I bet we can get them to work. Cooking will certainly be easier if we don't have to sit everything directly in the coals."

The fire flamed a bit, heralding the entrance of the woodcutters on a cold gust of air.

"Ahh, does it feel good in here," Joe exclaimed. He put his stack of wood down in one corner, then crossed to Marilyn.

"Good lord!" she squeaked when he gave her a hug, nuzzling his reddened nose against her neck. "You're as frozen as a snowman!"

She twisted in his arms and put her hands against his cheeks, then shook her head in mock exasperation. She glanced over at the two boys. "I hope you didn't chop off any fingers or toes. Until you thaw out, you wouldn't even feel their loss."

"Man, you should have seen Alex. He never chopped wood before today, but he did real good!"

"Did you save a chip?" Marilyn asked as she pulled Joe's hat off.

"Yeah, right here." Alex produced the chip. "Robbie said I have to carve something out of it."

"Is that an old custom of some sort?" Charles asked. He stepped forward, nearer the circle that had formed in front of the fireplace.

Joe shrugged out of his heavy coat. "I don't know how old it is. My grandparents celebrated every 'first.' First tooth. First step. First word and every other first. Each of their kids had a little treasure box for all kinds of 'first' mementos. My folks did the same for us, and now we do the same for ours." He reached down to tousle Lucy's hair. "I thought we'd never get a lock from this one's head."

Jennifer peered at Lucy. "You've never cut your hair?"

" 'Course I have. Mom cut my bangs when I was eight." She poked out her lower lip and blew out a puff that lifted her bangs. She grinned when they fell back in a straight silky line. "They saved my first tooth, too. Gross, huh?"

Jennifer switched her gaze to her mother. "Do you have my first tooth? Or hair from my first haircut?"

Charles answered. "Of course we do. In your baby book. Don't we, Jude?"

Judith lifted her gaze to his. "Yes, of course we do."

"That *is* gross," Alex interjected. But for once his grin was good-natured. "Watch out, Lucy. Jenn invents her own rules in Monopoly."

"I do not."

"You guys want to play?" Lucy asked. She scooted over to make room for them to sit. "We can start again, can't we, Jennifer?"

Jennifer stared up at her brother, then over at Robbie, who was already shedding his coat and crossing to them. "Sure," she finally said. She edged over as well, then followed Lucy's lead by collecting the paper money and redistributing it in four equal piles.

Charles stared at the scene before him. The four children gathered around the low table, amicably jostling for the most comfortable positions. They took the pillows Judith handed them, then settled down to the serious business of rolling the dice.

Joe and Marilyn sat on the hearth and talked quietly while Joe tested the coffee sitting in a pot to the side. He started to tuck a loose strand of Marilyn's hair behind her ear, but stopped first to wipe the soot from his hand before finishing the gesture.

Charles looked away and met Judith's hooded gaze. He shifted from his left foot to his right. Finally he moved to one of the couches.

"Why don't you come sit over here," he began, indicating the couch. "It'll be warmer."

"I've got this spot all heated up," she answered after only a brief hesitation. "There's a comforter behind you."

"That's okay."

There was an awkward silence between them that even the children's chatter and the Walkers' quiet conversation could not disguise. He felt defeated already. But with no alternative—no other rooms warm enough to retreat to and no phone or television for distraction—Charles sat down on one of the couches. Just beyond his feet Lucy was perched on her knees, shaking the dice in her hands, trying to talk the plastic cubes into the best pattern for her.

"Six. Yes!" She moved her piece forward with six enthusiastic jabs.

"Marvin Gardens. Don't waste your money on it," Robbie advised her. "I already own one of the yellow ones, and Alex has the other. It doesn't do you any good to buy it."

Charles leaned forward. "No real estate investment is ever a bad idea. If nothing else, you can always trade it. I guarantee, before this game is done, someone will want it."

Lucy looked over her shoulder at him and grinned. "All right. I'll buy it."

Robbie and Alex both groaned, but Jennifer laughed. "My dad knows everything about real estate."

"Real estate?" Lucy asked.

"Yeah. You know, buying land and buildings and stuff. Just like in Monopoly. Only he builds *real* hotels."

At her boastful words, Joe looked up. "A real estate developer? I guess business must be a little down these days."

Charles relaxed back on the couch. "For some people, maybe. But a tight economy doesn't have to be a curse. There's always a good deal waiting to be made if you're smart. The people who lose out are the short-term players. If you plan for the long haul, you'll always come out to the good."

Joe nodded and glanced at the game board as Alex rolled the dice and moved his piece. "We bought nineteen acres a long time ago. North of Edgard. Built a dome first, then later on we built a bigger house."

"A dome?" Charles grinned. This family was even stranger than he'd thought.

"Yeah." Joe looked at him with a patient expression, much like a tolerant parent gives a difficult child. "We built it in one long weekend with the help of a lot of friends. I'm sure you can appreciate the fact that for less than two thousand dollars we built almost a thousand square feet of space that's still in use twenty years later. With only routine upkeep, I might add."

Charles studied the other man. "Not a bad return on your investment. Too bad I can't get free labor for the new hotel, eh, Jude? 'Course, I don't think the Neighborhood Preservation Center would go for a dome anyway."

It irritated Charles to no end that the man's tolerant expression did not change, except, perhaps, to become a trifle amused. What in the hell did an old hippie who lived in a dome find amusing about him? He lived in a mansion in the finest neighborhood available. He employed close to a hundred people and kept over five hundred construction workers busy on a pretty regular basis. All this guy did was live in the boondocks and sell cheap art.

"A dome isn't for everyone," Joe agreed. "Have you ever been in one?"

"It's cool," Robbie threw in. "You can stand in a certain spot and just whisper, and someone in another certain spot can hear you really well."

"It feels like you're inside the world. Like inside a globe," Lucy chimed in. "Mom's big loom is in China. Dad's easels are in California, and the wood stove is in the Middle East."

"That's 'cause it's the hot spot of the world right now," Robbie explained. "Hey, it's my turn." He took the dice from Jennifer. "Anyway, you guys should come visit us one day. You'd like the dome a lot."

"We have our own swimming hole, too," Lucy added.

"We have a swimming pool," Jennifer replied. "And a three-car garage and a *huge* rec room in the basement."

"A wreck room?" Lucy asked. "What's that?"

There was an uncomfortable silence in the room and Charles felt a stab of guilt. Jennifer sounded like a little braggart. He probably did, too. But dammit, Joe Walker had a patronizing way of looking at a person.

It was Alex who broke the awkward silence. "It's short for a recreation room. Are the acoustics in that dome good for playing music?"

Marilyn answered him. "It depends. It's probably

better for quiet types of music than for amplified sounds. What do you play?"

"He's a heavy-metal freak," Jennifer piped up.

"Shut up, dork."

"Well, you are."

"Heavy metal," Joe mused. "Like Metallica, Aerosmith, Alice Cooper."

"Skid Row, Guns N' Roses, Whitesnake," Alex added.

"Whitesnake. Who's that guy that plays guitar for them? Steve something . . ."

"Steve Vai." Alex stared at Joe with a surprised expression on his face. "You like Whitesnake?"

Joe started laughing. "I admit that heavy metal's not my first choice. But there's some real talent there. Especially Steve Vai. The man *can* play a guitar."

"Alex has a Steve Vai poster over his bed," Jennifer said as she threw the dice. "He *loves* Steve Vai. He wants to *be* Steve Vai!"

"Hey, my room is off limits to you. How do you know what posters I have?"

"A bunch of long-haired scuzzballs," she replied. Then, realizing what she'd said, she stared guiltily at Joe.

"I take it you don't like longhairs," he said, pulling his own long ponytail from behind his back. "You think I should cut this off?"

Jennifer's gaze veered to her mother, then her father, and finally even to her brother. But she received no help from anyone. She peeked tentatively at Joe. "Well, I didn't mean you. You even said you don't like heavy metal music all *that* much."

"What I like was what came before heavy metal. Acid rock. Jimi Hendrix. Vanilla Fudge."

"You mean Vanilla Ice?" Jennifer exclaimed. "*You* like Vanilla Ice?"

Everyone started laughing at that. Everyone except Charles. Who, or what, was a Vanilla Ice? he wondered. It sounded like a dessert. But he refused to ask. He would sound too ignorant.

"No, no. I'm not really a Vanilla Ice fan, Jennifer. But I think every kind of music, including rap, has its place. You've got to remember that music has always been an expression of culture. All art is. Just because a particular style of music is foreign to our cultural knowledge doesn't mean it's not valid. In fact, music and all the other forms of art are mankind's finest means of learning about one another."

Alex and Jennifer were staring at Joe Walker in amazement. Judith also seemed fascinated by his words. In contrast, Lucy and Robbie were completely unaffected. No doubt Joe expounded like this all the time to them.

"What's the cultural significance of heavy metal music?" Charles asked. He knew at once his tone was too strident, but he couldn't help it. This guy irritated the hell out of him.

"Those who write it, perform it, and listen to it obviously enjoy it. Perhaps they're angry with the status quo. Perhaps their childhoods were troubled or unhappy, and now they view the whole world as an extension of their parents. They're expecting the worst from life because maybe that's been their main experience."

"Is that supposed to forgive satanism and all those rituals—they had unhappy childhoods?"

The game had stopped and now everyone was staring at Charles. He hadn't meant to sound so angry. Judith shifted nervously in her chair and both of his children were clearly uncomfortable. But he couldn't back out now.

"Everyone has a less-than-ideal childhood, somehow or other," Joe replied. "I'm sure our somewhat nomadic lifestyle will leave its marks on our children —both good and bad. The thing is, they're all three very different individuals. Robbie will probably be a real settled sort. He'll dig his roots in deep wherever he finally lives. Lucy is an adventuress. She'll probably find North America far too confining. As for Josie." He gazed fondly at the sleeping child. "I'm not sure, but she'll probably be our scientist. Her boundless curiosity may very well lead her into the world of science, or something like that."

He gave Charles a keen look, then glanced at Alex. "You like heavy metal. Are you a satanist?"

"No!" Charles answered for Alex before the boy could. At once Alex's face clouded over.

"How would you know?"

"Alex!" Judith jerked upright.

He sent her a furious glare. "I'm not a satanist. That's too ridiculous for words. But even if I was— even if I burned dissected animals in my room—he wouldn't know. He doesn't know anything about me!"

He leaped up from the floor and stormed away. Charles wanted to storm away, too. To hide from all the eyes that were now riveted upon him. But it was useless. The damage was done. The imperfections of their family life had been laid whole before these people—these self-righteous strangers. And now, bohemians though they were—gypsies—they would be even more smug.

Joe cleared his throat, but it was Marilyn who broke the awful silence.

"I think the hardest part of being a parent is accepting that our children are growing into people quite separate from us. They don't need us as much as they once did."

Charles was trembling inside, but there was a soothing quality in Marilyn Walker's voice. "Is it wrong to hope you've imparted a decent set of values to your kids?" he asked bitterly. He stared up the curtained-off stairs, where Alex had disappeared.

"He probably has those values. Mom, the flag, and apple pie aren't exclusive to the penny loafers and Dockers crowd, you know."

If Joe Walker had said that, Charles's temper would have boiled out of control. But coming from the soft-spoken Marilyn, the words served to deepen his depression. Was he being unfair to Alex? At that moment he honestly didn't know.

"Well," Jennifer interrupted. "What do we do with all of Alex's properties? Do we divide them up or give them to the bank, or what?"

"Maybe you could go convince him to come back," Lucy suggested.

"Are you kidding? No way. When he gets mad he won't talk to anyone. He just plays his guitar."

"Well, I guess we should just put his property back in the bank and keep on playing without him."

The game resumed, but not with nearly the same level of enthusiasm as before. Charles retreated into a *National Geographic* article about an archaeological dig in Greenland. But he remained acutely aware of the movements of everyone. Marilyn pulled out some yarn from her pocket and began to crochet—at least he thought it was crocheting. Judith closed her eyes again, although he was sure she was not asleep.

Joe checked little Josie's brow and murmured to Marilyn that she felt cooler. Then he disappeared up the stairs.

Probably going to seek out Alex, Charles thought sourly. Yet he could not pretend any longer about the root of his irritation with Joe Walker. He was jealous, plain and simple. The man connected with Alex in a way he himself never had—at least not in recent years.

He stared hard at a picture of a Norseman, frozen for centuries, but the ancient features did not really register in his mind. Instead he saw the picture from his desk. Himself with Alex, Judith, and baby Jennifer. Alex had thought his dad the most important man in the world back then. Now, even though Charles knew he'd simply been a small-time contractor struggling to keep his business afloat, it seemed maybe he had been more important than he'd known.

He peered again at Judith. Her eyes were open now but she was staring blankly at the ceiling.

He'd been more important to her, too. Despite their struggles back then, she'd never talked of leaving him.

He let the magazine fall to his lap, and closed his eyes. The fire crackled in the hearth. The three children's voices were quiet as they rolled the dice and moved their pieces on the Monopoly board.

"Uh, Lucy. Would you consider selling me Marvin Gardens?" Robbie asked his sister sheepishly.

Charles heard her giggle. "You were right, Mr. Montgomery," she called to Charles. Then she turned to her brother. "Sure, I'll sell it to you. But it's gonna cost you plenty."

Chapter *Seven*

Joe Walker came down the stairs with a rather battered-looking guitar. There was little conversation in the room as he fiddled with the instrument, tuning it and strumming a few chords while he hummed under his breath. The mood of the room was decidedly subdued. But then, being confined to one room with eight other people for the duration of a blizzard was enough to subdue anyone, Judith thought. Seven, she amended as she once more looked at the red bedspread that curtained off the stairwell, preventing the loss of precious heat to the upstairs.

Alex was still up there. He must be freezing.

She glanced over at Charles. Why didn't he go up after Alex? She knew, however, that Alex would never come down at his father's request. Maybe if he ordered, but not if he asked.

How had their relationship become so skewed? Most kids would balk at the order but consent to the request. But Charles and Alex were embroiled in a classic power play, or so she realized from her women's roundtable group. Charles demanded that Alex be what he expected of a son—to look and act, and even think like a younger version of himself. Meanwhile, Alex was equally determined to be just the opposite.

From the corner of her eye she saw Josie shift in her make-do bed. Her eyes opened, revealing a wide and blurry blue gaze. For a moment she appeared frightened. Clearly she did not remember where she was. Then her mother bent over her, and her rosy cheeks relaxed in a smile.

"Hi, sugar. How are you feeling?" Marilyn touched her palm to the child's brow. "No fever," she murmured to her husband. Then she picked up Josie, blanket and all, and settled down into the chair with the little girl in her lap.

"I had a funny dream, Mama," Josie said as she cuddled in her mother's embrace. "We were in the most beautiful place you ever saw. It was soft and warm. And it smelled good."

"When we get home Moonbeam can tell you what your dream meant," Lucy said. She got up from the game and knelt before her sister. "Want to help me beat them in Monopoly? You can roll the dice for me."

Josie smiled, but shook her head no.

"Can I get you something, puddin'?" Joe asked.

"Are you hungry or thirsty? Do you need to go to the bathroom?"

Again she shook her head. "Everybody in my dream was so nice. There was a gate to keep out all the bad people."

"Well, there're no bad people here," Marilyn answered.

The child frowned in concentration. "Is it still Christmastime?"

"Of course it is, honey. You've only been asleep a little while."

"Well, where's the Christmas tree?"

The other three children looked up from their board game.

"Yeah. We need a Christmas tree."

"We can cut one down."

"We *have* to have a Christmas tree."

Joe laughed and laid the old guitar aside. "You're right. We *do* need a Christmas tree." He reached for his coat.

"Shouldn't you wait until it stops snowing?" Judith asked.

"I doubt it's going to stop snowing, at least not today. Robbie and I will just go out past the driveway. We won't go out of sight of the house."

"Can't I go too, Daddy?" Lucy implored.

"If it weren't snowing so bad I'd say yes. But those drifts are probably getting pretty deep. They might be over your head in some places."

She frowned in disappointment, but did not pout as Judith knew Jennifer would have.

"We can get the ornaments ready," Jennifer said. "Do you know where they are, Mom?"

"In the basement," Charles answered.

Joe looked at him while buttoning up his jacket. "Want to join us?"

"I'll help," Alex interrupted before Charles could reply. He pushed past the curtain, already dressed in coat and hat. His nose was red from the cold upper floor of the house, Judith saw. And he deliberately avoided his father's eyes.

Joe paused and glanced again at Charles. So did Judith. She saw him stiffen at Alex's entrance, and though there was no physical manifestation of it, she sensed his emotional withdrawal. Joe must have recognized it as well, for without further word he headed for the kitchen, followed by both boys.

"Well." Marilyn squeezed Josie close. "Looks like you've set the ball rolling, sweetheart. I better start some lunch, though, because they're going to be hungry—and cold. Shall we make sandwiches and soup, Judith?"

"That sounds good. I'll help."

"Terrific. Girls, come with us. You can get those ornaments." Then Marilyn looked at Charles. "Do you think you could watch Josie?"

Charles appeared lost in thought—unpleasant thoughts, judging by the expression on his face. But at Marilyn's request he looked up. "Watch Josie? Uh, sure. Sure. I can do that."

He stood up and crossed to the couch adjacent to them. When he sat down, Marilyn stood up and, to his obvious surprise, placed Josie squarely in his lap.

"We won't be in the kitchen long," she said with a smile. "Thanks."

Judith could barely stifle her amusement as she and Marilyn entered the frigid kitchen. Charles had not held a little child like that in years. He could handle powerful bankers, union bosses, and irate contractors with grace and assurance. Yet just now he'd looked completely undone. And all because of one five-year-old girl.

"They'll do fine together," Marilyn said. "Josie is at that age—you know—precocious and yet still innocent."

"She's an adorable child. All your children are delightful."

"Why, thank you. So are your two."

Judith pursed her lips ruefully as she headed for the pantry. "No, delightful is hardly the word for my two. They're smart and talented. And they can be funny and entertaining, and sometimes even charming. But not for long." She swallowed past a lump that had formed in her throat. "They fight over everything—with each other and with us. I . . . I sometimes think Charles's business success has been unfortunate—at least for them."

They were quiet a moment as they gathered pots and utensils, bowls and mugs. Judith found several cans of soup while Marilyn put bread, cheese, butter, and milk on a tray. From the basement door they could hear Lucy and Jennifer exclaiming and laughing as they searched for the Christmas ornaments.

"It doesn't take much to keep kids happy," Marilyn said. "It's important that they have a sense of accomplishment. They need to know that, despite a few failures now and again, there *are* things they can do. And of course, they need to always know they're loved."

Judith busied herself with soup spoons and napkins. "I love my children. So does Charles. But . . ." She trailed off, uneasy with what she was revealing to this stranger. Even in her women's group she'd not faced the possibility of her own failings. She had discussed her marriage and its shortcomings, but never her mothering. She'd always considered herself a good mother. But how good was she when she could see the difference between her own "well-brought-up" children and this woman's—and see how much worse her children came out in comparison?

"For all the things they have, I guess they're not that happy," she finished in a whisper.

"We found them, Mom!" Jennifer's shout drifted up from below.

"She certainly sounds happy right now," Marilyn offered with a generous smile.

Judith sighed. "This is all an adventure for her. New entertainment."

Marilyn shrugged, then lifted her tray. "Life's always an adventure. You can find entertainment everywhere. New people, new places." She laughed. "There's that gypsy side of me, I'm afraid. I forget that such a nomadic existence isn't for everyone."

The girls came up the stairs amid much excited chatter. As they staggered into the kitchen carrying a large cardboard box decorated with wreaths and Santa faces, the women's topic of conversation was necessarily abandoned. But Judith replayed it in her mind. Marilyn professed to be a gypsy at heart, yet she seemed to be a well-grounded person, sensible and straightforward. Judith had always thought of herself as the sensible sort—uncomplicated and practical. But perhaps there was that buried part of her that wished for freedom. Why else was she so dissatisfied with her life, the very sort of life that was envied by the rest of the world?

She shook her head as she set her tray down on the coffee table near the hearth. She couldn't explain or even understand it. She only knew that she was restless and unhappy.

Or perhaps she was unhappy and therefore restless.

It was not a truly earth-shattering realization, yet for Judith it had a profound effect. Her restlessness was founded in her unhappiness, not the other way around. If she were happy she would feel settled once more. Just having that bit of self-knowledge was extremely comforting.

She stood up and looked over at Charles. He still sat on the couch with Josie in his lap, and his face still held that disconcerted expression.

"How big is your hotel?" the child was asking.

"Thirty-three floors."

The girl looked doubtful. "Thirty-three? Thirty-three! Why so big?"

"Well, lots of people travel to New York, and they need a place to stay while they're visiting."

Josie frowned. "Do you have to cut down all the trees? In Edgard we don't let people cut down too many trees."

Charles smiled and even patted her arm. "There are no trees in this place. Just a bunch of old rotten buildings."

"Doesn't anybody live there?"

"Well, yes. But they'll move someplace else."

Marilyn busied herself with preparing the meal. Jennifer and Lucy had opened the box of decorations, but Judith could not tear herself away from the conversation between Charles and little Josie. In his arms she appeared more a fairy child than a gypsy child. A golden-haired angel of a child. But child that she was, she was nonetheless able to understand what Charles was saying, and it clearly troubled her.

"But . . . but what if they don't want to move?"

Charles shifted her in his arms. "But they will want to. Their houses are all . . . all yucky," he finished, obviously hoping his choice of words would convince her.

She considered for a moment. "My aunt Moonbeam's house is kind of yucky sometimes, but she still doesn't want to move. How do you *know* these people really want to move?"

Judith could tell that Charles's patience was wearing thin. "I just know," he said curtly. "Why don't you go help the other girls look at all the Christmas ornaments?"

He lifted her off his lap and set her on her feet before him. But her serious expression never changed, and her solemn stare did not waver from his face. "I hope you never build a hotel in Edgard," she said slowly.

Judith's eyes veered from Josie to Charles, and then back to the child. Though only five years old, the little girl seemed at that moment infinitely wise. How astounding was the clear logic of a child, unencumbered by the rationalizations that came with maturity. Josie had cut to the heart of the real estate dilemma, and to Judith's amazement she was making Charles Montgomery squirm.

Charles cleared his throat. "Edgard is too small a town for one of my hotels."

"Good. I love my house and my room and my yard and my treehouse. I don't want a great big giant building to come and crash it all to pieces."

Jennifer looked up from spreading ornaments out on the floor. "My dad's buildings are real nice, Josie. I bet you'd like them if you saw them."

"Hotels aren't as important as houses," Lucy threw in. "My dad says if more people owned their own homes, then there wouldn't be so many slums."

"Why did he say that?" Judith could not help but ask, although she was as surprised at her question as Charles obviously was.

Lucy shrugged. "He says people always take good care of what belongs to them. If everybody owned their own houses, then I guess they would all take care of them—you know, pick up the litter and mow the grass and stuff like that. Then the cities would all be nice places to live."

"Not every place has grass to grow," Charles said testily. "Cities are very different from small towns."

"Yes, they certainly are," Marilyn interjected. She crossed over to Josie and picked her up. With her arms around her young child, a gentle smile on her face, and her longish hair coming loose from its braid, Marilyn Walker looked the essence of motherhood. Judith recognized it at once and it brought a pang of wistfulness to her heart.

Charles saw it, too, and it stilled his next words. He did not wish to argue the benefits of real estate development with a five-year-old and her mother. Especially when the two of them presented such a perfect picture of maternal love.

Norman Rockwell would have loved them, Charles thought ruefully, for despite their lifestyle—so outside the mainstream of American life—they still somehow epitomized everything that was considered truly American. He couldn't understand it until Marilyn planted a kiss in Josie's curly hair. Then he knew. The Walkers were a perfect example of the family unit—of family love and togetherness. Though they were itinerant artists, they were nonetheless the basic unit of American life: a happy, wholesome family.

They were, and he and his family were not.

He blinked hard and swallowed, then forced himself to look away. Judith was staring at him with a strange expression on her face. The two other girls were busy with the ornaments, but as the silence continued Lucy looked up, and then so did Jennifer.

Charles cleared his throat nervously, then forced a chuckle. "We should be talking more about building up the fire instead of building hotels." He walked over to the pile of wood and picked up three good-sized logs. Once he thrust them in the fireplace and had them placed just so, he dusted off his hands and looked at Judith. "How's lunch coming?"

Judith started, as if his words had jolted her from unhappy thoughts of her own. "Um. It's almost ready. Right, Marilyn?"

Marilyn studied Judith as she ran her hand absently through Josie's curls. "You know what? I want to take Josie to the bathroom." Her gaze shifted to Charles. "Could you help Judith finish lunch?"

It was cooler by the dining table, for it was across the room from the fireplace. But overall the big living room was warming up. Charles spread out the tablecloth Judith gave him, then began to set out plates and glasses while she put soup to heat in a pot hanging above the fire.

"Just put the mayonnaise, mustard, and other condiments out so everyone can make their sandwiches the way they want, then spread out the bread, meat, cheese, and lettuce on those two platters," she added as she folded napkins and placed the utensils out. Then she disappeared into the curtained-off kitchen to get milk.

Charles straightened a plate and pulled two bowls nearer their respective glasses. He was still oppressed by his terrible realization, though his rational self knew he should not be. After all, he'd planned this Christmas journey for the very purpose of addressing his family's problems. But somehow, seeing a family like the Walkers—so out of step with the rest of the world economically, and yet so solid emotionally—struck him to the heart. They were salt in his wounds, and though he knew it was a childish reaction, he hated them for it.

No, he decided as he glanced over at Jennifer and Lucy. It wasn't hate. The emotion that gripped him was far nearer to envy, and it sat most uncomfortably with him.

"Oh! Give me that one!" Jennifer exclaimed, drawing her father's attention. As he watched, she snatched a heart-shaped ornament from Lucy's hands and held it up to admire.

"That one's mine, Jenny. Give it back," Lucy asked.

"No. I want it. When I hang this heart it will be a symbol of my love for Brett Franklin. It'll stop Sara Smythe from getting him while I'm gone."

"I had it first," Lucy insisted, reaching for the fragile ornament.

"Too bad," Jennifer snapped, jerking her hand back. But the ornament slipped from her grasp. With a tiny crash, it shattered on the coffee table. Jennifer gasped. "Just look what you made me do!"

"*I* didn't make you drop it. You did that all on your own."

"If you hadn't tried to grab it—"

"You grabbed it from me!" Lucy shouted back, her patience clearly come to an end. She stood up, scowling. "You're just one of those gimme, gimme girls. Selfish and mean. Always wanting things their way. And always blaming other people for everything."

Jennifer stared up at the younger girl who, up to now, had been quiet and malleable. She glanced at her father, then stood up too. But as she did so, she put one hand on the table. At once she howled in pain.

"Oh! I'm cut. I'm cut!" She held her left hand up, then started to cry in earnest. "Daddy! I'm bleeding!"

Precisely at that moment everyone else returned. Marilyn came down the stairs with Josie. Judith hurried in from the kitchen, and Joe and the boys entered on a blast of icy air.

"Look at this beauty," Alex's excited voice carried over the sudden bedlam.

"I'm bleeding!" Jennifer howled.

"What in heaven's name?" Judith exclaimed.

"What happened?" Marilyn hurried to Jennifer's side.

"It's all Lucy's fault!" Jennifer accused through her loud sobs. With tears streaming down her face and pricks of blood on her hand, she looked every part the wounded victim.

For her part, Lucy was no less adamant. Her straight dark hair seemed almost to crackle with indignation as she faced her accuser. "*She* grabbed the ornament from me. *She* dropped it. Then *she* put her own hand down on the broken glass."

"That sounds like our Jennifer," Alex quipped. "Greedy *and* stupid."

"Mama," Jennifer wailed, turning into her mother's waiting arms.

Marilyn and Judith stared at the sobbing girl. So did Robbie and young Josie. But Joe Walker was looking straight at Charles.

Once more Charles felt a grating anger. But he also felt an uncomfortable sense of guilt. It had happened just as Lucy had said. Jennifer had caused the entire mess, but she didn't want to take the blame. It was a pattern of hers that he suddenly recognized well.

"I'll handle this," he said. There was a certain security to be had in taking charge of the situation, even if in the final analysis it was your child—and your family—who came off the poorer.

"You shouldn't have grabbed the ornament from Lucy. Anyway, those cuts don't look all that bad," he snapped.

"They're only scratches," Judith confirmed, locking eyes with her husband.

"Good. Why don't you go wash up, Jenny, while your mother cleans up the glass."

Jennifer stared at him through damp eyes. When it was clear to her that no sympathy would be forthcoming from him, she turned back to her mother.

But Judith forestalled any further outburst from Jennifer with a stern look. "The hand washing can wait until after *you* clean up the glass," she stated. "Don't argue with me, Jennifer. Just hurry up and do it. And be thorough. Now"—she turned toward Marilyn—"I'm sure everyone must be starving."

Why did he always manage to say the wrong thing

with Judith? Charles brooded a short time later as he bit into a ham-and-Swiss sandwich. Conversation was quiet and desultory, but he felt a depression that would not go away. His daughter had made him feel foolish, like an inadequate parent. Then Judith had made him feel even worse by overriding his instructions. She was right—Jennifer *should* clean up her own mess. But Judith had made it seem as though he were an insensitive husband, always pushing the dirty work off on his wife. Everyone who knew him knew he treated her like a queen. She had a housekeeper and a maid. Plus the groundskeeper. Yet she still managed to make him feel like a fool—a failure as a husband.

He swallowed only with the greatest difficulty and looked across the table at Alex. In contrast to Jennifer, who was sulking, and Judith, who was concentrating on her meal, Alex was more animated than Charles could ever recall. He and Robbie were laughing and joking like old friends, and even though Joe did no more than nod or laugh every now and again, it was clear he was as much a part of Alex's good spirits as anyone.

"I still think that forked tree would have made a more interesting Christmas tree," Alex said, gesturing with his spoon. "Just imagine. Two stars. Or better yet, Santa on one and a star on the other. You know, the two sides of Christmas."

"You could start a new trend." Robbie laughed. "I can see it now. Alex's Forked Christmas Tree Lot. And if you sold ornaments, you'd really clean up. People would need twice as many of them."

Everyone laughed except Charles and Jennifer, although she did look a little interested.

"That's a thought-provoking point," Joe said. He reached for more bread. "Christmas in America does have two distinct sides. Like you said, Alex, there's the birth of Jesus, and then there's Santa Claus."

"Christmas is like a big birthday party," Lucy said. "It's Jesus' birthday, only everyone gets presents."

"Shouldn't we give Jesus something back?"

At Judith's question, everyone turned to stare at her. "Well," she continued. "Isn't that what the Christmas spirit actually is? Spreading goodwill to all of mankind in His name?"

"You're right, of course. It's too bad we couldn't all continue to give that gift the entire year through," Marilyn said.

"I rather doubt most people will give up that Santa side of Christmas," Charles remarked. "Everyone wants their gifts on Christmas morning. Besides, the retailing industry would collapse without Christmas. We'd have an economic disaster on our hands."

He bit into his sandwich with extra force. What a naive and self-righteous bunch they all were. Was he the only realist in the group?

"You can combine the two," Marilyn stated in a gentle, nonjudgmental tone. "Every salesclerk and shopgirl who works on commission needs that Christmas shopping frenzy. Besides, there's nothing in the world to compete with the joy a parent feels watching their children Christmas morning. My point is that spreading happiness in whatever way we do it—and whatever season of the year we choose to do it in—is the gift we give to the baby Jesus. We just need to remember to do it the whole year long."

She was right, of course, and Charles knew it. But

a devil seemed to goad him to challenge her words. "I'm sure my kids would love me to spread even more happiness their way—and thereby spread more money their way. Retailers would love it, too," he added sarcastically.

Marilyn looked at him with a patient expression on her face. "Perhaps they'd like something from you that money can't buy."

There was an awkward silence. To Charles's relief —and amazement—it was Alex who stepped in to fill it.

"Like permission to quit school and become a full-time musician?" he suggested hopefully. But he laughed as he said it, and even Charles could not be angry.

"Like taking me mountain climbing," Robbie said with a meaningful look at his mother.

Marilyn grimaced. "When you're older," she replied. "When you're older."

"Marilyn is afraid of heights," Joe explained. "Even driving through the mountains is an ordeal for her." He reached out to grasp her hand. "Robbie, on the other hand, has no fear of heights whatsoever."

Marilyn gave her son a mock glare. "When he helped his father repair the roof, I had to leave the house. It was just too traumatic for me."

"Oh, Mom. I did fine. Dad told you I was really careful."

"I know. I know. But it's so high and steep. And accidents *can* happen. Just look at how we skidded yesterday. If it weren't for that tree on the side of the road, we might have gone right over—" She broke off with a shudder.

"Well, we're all safe now, so don't worry about it," Joe reassured her.

Charles concentrated on his meal as conversation continued on around him. Judith was slowly drawn in. Jennifer abandoned her sulky mood as well, pulled against her will into the warm banter among the Walkers. Only Charles held himself apart. Though he ate, it was only to maintain a semblance of normality. In fact, his stomach was knotted with conflicting emotions.

Joe Walker's wife adored him. His children loved him and listened to him. They *wanted* to do things with him. Now Alex had fallen under his spell, and judging by Jennifer's laughter, so had she.

Charles stole a glance at Judith, then swiftly looked back at his plate. She was smiling too, involved in a lively conversation about the merits of a school voucher system. When had she decided vouchers were a good idea?

A part of him—the rational part—knew that his family rarely shared a meal as absent of conflict as this one was. This was exactly what he had wanted for his family. But at the same time, he knew this amiable atmosphere was not due to him. The truth was, it existed in spite of him.

For a moment he wondered if *he* was the problem, if *he* was the cause of his family's disharmony. Yet if it were not for his insistence, they would not even be here. No, he was the only one of them actively *seeking* some sort of solution for all their problems.

But as Alex broke into an impromptu version of the Chipmunks singing "All I Want for Christmas Is My Two Front Teeth," causing everyone else to dissolve into laughter, Charles could not escape the sinking feeling that no matter how hard he tried, he could never re-create the happy scene before him.

Never.

Chapter Eight

"**D**addy."

Charles looked up automatically at Josie's plaintive call, even though he was not her father. There was something in her worried tone that wouldn't allow him just to sit and stare at the open book before him any longer. Joe also looked up from his spot near the hearth surrounded by the other four children. Robbie and Alex were carving. Lucy and Jennifer—friends again—were stringing popcorn, all the while offering the boys free advice on their efforts.

"It looks sort of like somebody's ear," Jennifer stated.

Alex looked up at her, but his reply was mild. "It would have to be a really deformed ear." He held it against his head so that it poked out through his hair.

"You've gotta have two," Robbie advised. "*I* gotta have two. Would you make me a pair just like that?"

They all laughed.

"Here. Catch," Lucy ordered. She threw one kernel of popped corn at each boy, but despite their diving efforts with mouths opened wide, the popcorn fell short of its goal. She laughed. "Okay, second try." But this time she threw a handful at each of them.

Amidst all their good-natured shoving and scrambling for the popcorn, Joe rose and crossed to Josie's side.

"What's the trouble, sweetheart?"

Charles watched as she took her father's hand, then climbed up into his lap. "Roger Rabbit is still sick. She won't eat or drink or anything."

Joe pressed a kiss into her tousled curls as they both gazed down into the box at the injured rabbit. "He was hurt pretty bad by that lynx, sugar. It might take him a long time to get better."

"She's a girl," Josie corrected him. Then she stared up at him, her face solemn. "What if she can't get better?"

Joe hesitated. He glanced up, meeting Charles's gaze. In that moment Charles recognized that for all his relaxed ways with both his children and Charles's, the man did not have all the answers. There was no easy way to respond to a question like Josie's. Not when the questioner stared at you with such an innocent, trusting face. He was glad the task didn't fall to him.

"If she doesn't get better, then I guess she'll go up to heaven."

Josie digested that a moment. "To heaven? With the baby Jesus?"

Joe nodded. "As I recall, Jesus especially loved animals and little children."

Stupid move, Charles thought with undeniable relish. He should never have mentioned little children.

As Charles expected, Josie's eyes widened with fear. "Jesus wants little children in heaven, too? But . . . but I don't *want* to be dead!"

Joe hugged her tighter. "Now, now. You don't have to worry about that, sweetheart. You're staying here with your mom and dad and brother and sister. But you know what? You don't have to be afraid of heaven. Remember when Moonbeam and her kids moved last year? Summer and Spring were both afraid they'd hate their new home and that they'd never make any new friends. But guess what—now they love their new home and they have a bunch of new friends.

"Well, heaven is like that. It's like moving to a new neighborhood. Before you get there it seems really scary. But once you're there, well, it turns out to be a pretty neat place."

Everyone had stopped to listen. Josie looked from her father down to the ailing rabbit, pondering his explanation. Charles glanced at his own children and was surprised by the thoughtful expressions on their faces. Religion was not a subject often discussed in their household. They knew about Jesus, of course, about heaven and hell, and Christmas and Easter. But not in personal terms. Death had not touched them in any close way.

"If she goes to heaven . . ." Josie trailed off, trying to figure things out. "Will her leg still hurt her up in heaven?"

Joe shook his head. "No, it won't hurt."

"Will she have any friends there?"

"I bet there're lots of other rabbits already there."

The little girl sighed, and Charles felt her relief as profoundly as his own. "I hope she doesn't go to heaven, Daddy. But if she does, well, I guess that's okay, too."

"Do you really believe animals go to heaven?" Of all people, the question came from Alex.

"Of course they do," little Josie said. She stared at him as if daring him to deny it.

Joe smiled. "You know, I've always believed that heaven is our reward for living a good life on earth, and if that's so, then it must provide whatever makes us happiest. Can you imagine a happy existence without the beauty of animals and plants?"

"What would heaven be like for you, Alex?" Marilyn asked from her spot, curled up on one of the couches.

Alex thought a moment, holding the carving knife idly in his hand. He was getting big, Charles realized. Almost a man. Yet when he smiled shyly at Marilyn, then ducked his head in embarrassment, he was the same little boy dressed as an angel who had sung so loudly at that Christmas pageant those long years ago.

"Heaven would be filled with music," Alex began. "Not just church music—you know, pianos and organs and stuff like that."

"He wants to bring his electric guitar with him." Jennifer laughed, but instead of her usual mocking tone, Charles decided she actually sounded accepting of her brother.

Alex realized it also, for he shrugged and grinned. "Guitars, drums, amplifiers. Maybe God likes really loud music."

"He liked the little drummer boy," Judith offered. "Remember in the song? Baby Jesus smiled when the little drummer boy offered him the gift of his song."

Mother and son's eyes met, and watching from across the room, Charles felt a piercing emotion, a physical ache deep in his chest. Judith's love for their son fairly radiated from her, and Alex's returning emotion was just as apparent. It struck Charles in that moment that no one anywhere felt that way about him. It was a devastating realization.

"What would heaven have in it for you, Mom?"

At Alex's question, all eyes turned to Judith. For a moment she hesitated. Her eyes veered briefly to Charles, then just as quickly away. She shifted in her chair and finally smiled.

"Well, let's see. Heaven would have to have my parents—and eventually my children—"

"We know that," Jennifer interrupted. "We want to know what other things your heaven would have in it."

"That's not an easy question." Judith laughed. "Can I think about it a little while?"

"Well, I know what I want in heaven," Jennifer replied.

"Lots of stores?"

"Shut up, Alex," she said with a mock frown as everyone else laughed. "Okay, I *would* want lots of nice clothes . . ."

This time everyone howled. Despite her own gales

of laughter, however, Marilyn saved Jennifer. "It seems to me the Bible is full of references to fine robes and raiments of silk. So Jennifer isn't so far off the mark."

"You see?" Jennifer exclaimed. "It's not so funny after all."

"Okay," Joe said. "Heaven has to have animals and plants. Lots of music. Nice clothes," he added with a grin at Jennifer. "I know I want it to have great food. Corn bread. Baklava. Sugar peas. Bagels."

"That's a weird combination," Lucy said, making a face.

"Oh, yeah? Well, what would you want?"

The girl grinned. "Popsicles and . . . and lots of baseball diamonds!"

"You could be the first woman in the major leagues. The *real* major leagues!" Robbie added with a dramatic roll of his eyes upward.

"Yeah! Baseball in heaven."

"My dad used to play baseball when he was a kid," Jennifer said. "Didn't you, Dad?"

Charles nodded as all eyes turned to him. "That's right. I was pretty good in high school."

"What would heaven have in it for you, Charles?"

The question came from Marilyn. Charles looked over at her. Quiet, thoughtful—observant—Marilyn. He fiddled with the book in his hands and swallowed uncomfortably. He didn't give a damn about finding happiness in heaven. What he wanted was happiness now, here on earth with his family. He cleared his throat, but before he could think of a reply, Alex spoke.

"Get Dad a phone that never breaks down, that he

can take everywhere—even into blizzards—and still call the office, and he'll be in heaven. Right, Dad?"

The children all laughed, and their raucous byplay helped cover the fact that none of the adults did. Judith stared down at her hands. Joe and Marilyn stared at Charles, then turned automatically toward each other.

Charles sat there, the book still in his hands, but he was unaware of it. Was that what Alex thought? That a direct phone line to his office was the most important thing in the world to him? That it would be heaven for him?

Judith stood up and walked to the window. Beyond her the snow still fell in a solid white silence. Jennifer also arose, draping her popcorn garland in her outstretched hands, comparing it to Lucy's. Alex's attentions had returned to his carving, and he and Robbie were talking quietly as they worked.

Marilyn had closed her eyes and appeared to be dozing, while Joe sat back with Josie still in his lap.

"Tell me and Roger Rabbit a story, Daddy. It'll make her feel better."

"Okay." Joe pressed a hand to his daughter's brow, then kissed the top of her head. "Feeling better, sugar?"

The child nodded. "I feel fine. Tell me the story of Little Two Eyes. I like that one."

Lucy looked up from her popcorn. "Don't you want a Christmas story, Josie?"

Marilyn laughed, though her eyes remained closed. "You know your dad. He can make it into a Christmas story."

"Oh, yeah. Like he did 'The Three Bears' at Easter for her?"

"And 'Cinderella' at the birthday ball," Robbie added with a grin. "I bet I know what Little Two Eyes will want for Christmas."

"Hey, you guys. You're going to spoil the ending," Joe complained with a grin.

The story unfolded with frequent contributions from the audience. Even Alex and Jennifer, who had never heard the tale before, managed to throw in their own suggestions. Only Josie listened silently, her plump baby face set in serious concentration.

"Want to help us with a puzzle?" Judith asked. Charles looked up in surprise. She shrugged slightly and gestured toward Marilyn, who was opening up a puzzle box on the dining table.

"Come on, Charles. I bet you haven't worked a puzzle in years," Marilyn called.

He pushed up from the chair, wondering if Marilyn had urged Judith to include him, or if she'd done it on her own. "At least ten years, probably more. What do we have here?"

"It's Custer's Last Stand." Marilyn handed him the box cover. "Grisly, I know. But it's what we have."

All in all the afternoon proved to be strangely pleasant. Charles, Judith, and Marilyn worked on the puzzle, sometimes talking, sometimes not. Once Joe's Little Two Eyes was happily ensconced in a new home with parents who loved her—and her first Christmas tree—he joined the other adults at the puzzle.

By then Lucy and Jennifer had four long popcorn strands ready, so the children all tackled the tree trimming with glee.

Judith kept a nervous eye on the children's hilarity. "Oh, they're going to tip it over—"

"They'll do fine," Joe reassured her. "Here, I found another edge piece, with brown and red. Weren't you looking for pieces like this?"

"That's it," Judith crowed, connecting two long puzzle sections.

The tree was finished long before the puzzle was even halfway complete. The expensive red balls, meant to create an elegant, shimmering theme tree with tiny twinkling white lights, were softened by the generous loopings of the popcorn garlands. The children had put the strings of lights up just in case, in the hopes that the electricity would eventually return. But the firelight flickering off the variety of gleaming glass balls, coupled with the mixed scents of fir tree, wood smoke, and popcorn, lent the tree a wholesome charm that bewitched them all.

"Let's sing Christmas carols," Josie suggested as she gazed with delight at the tall tree.

"Wait. What about the star at the top of the tree?" Lucy reminded her.

"Here," Alex put in, handing Josie the large silvery star. "I'll hold you so you can put it up."

Josie hesitated only a moment. As she stepped up to Alex, her confidence in him obvious, Charles saw Alex smile. It was not a smile he'd seen often on his son's face—at least not in a long time.

He lifted Josie up high until she could reach the topmost tree branch. It took her a few tries to get the star securely in place. Once she nearly dropped it. But Alex held her steady, and when the star was up she gave him a bright smile.

"We did it! Isn't it beautiful?"

"It sure is, Josie. You did a great job." Alex held her

in his arms a few seconds longer. "You know, we need an expert tree trimmer like you back at our house."

"Isn't this your house?"

"No, we just came here for a Christmas vacation. But I'm glad we did," he added, giving her a little jiggle.

Charles stared hard at Alex, unable to quite believe what he'd heard. Alex was . . . well, he wasn't acting like himself. The tall boy holding the little girl seemed almost a stranger. But a good stranger. Then Josie spoke up again.

"I'm glad you came here, too, 'cause there weren't any other houses close to where we wrecked." A tiny frown crossed her face. "I hope our van is okay."

"C'mon, Josie. Who's gonna steal it in a blizzard?" Robbie said. "Boy, I'm sure glad we didn't have to camp out in the snow. That's no fun at all."

"What about your aunt Sunbeam?" Jennifer asked. "Doesn't she live in a tent, even in the winter?"

"Moonbeam," Lucy corrected her with a giggle. "Her name is Moonbeam. And anyway, her tepee is bigger and heavier than most tents. Plus, it has a fire in it."

"She knows how to put the tepee in places where the trees protect it from the wind," Robbie explained.

"And sometimes, when it's really too cold, she comes to stay with us," Josie finished.

Everyone laughed. "I hope she and her family are somewhere warm right now during this blizzard," Judith said. "It's still coming down pretty thick out there."

Despite the large spans of glass, the heavy cloud cover and steady snow brought an early dusk inside the house. Charles added wood to the fire while Mari-

lyn lit two kerosene lamps to keep the dark at bay. As
he looked over the living room, Charles was struck by
how different it appeared from yesterday. It was
crowded with furniture—and people. No essence remained of the elegantly composed decor that had appeared so magazine-picture perfect.

Judith had been right, he realized ruefully. It *had*
looked more like an office than a home. Now it looked
like a place people would want to live in: happy children at play; good smells; a comfortable sense of
closeness.

It was probably just the Christmas tree, he decided
as he closed the firescreen. But then Judith walked
by Alex and rumpled his hair, then touched Jennifer's arm in passing, and he knew it was more than
the tree. This enforced closeness might have been
hellish if they'd been left here alone, but the presence
of the Walkers had made it—

He paused, struggling to understand. Somehow
their presence had made it right.

He studied Joe and Marilyn, who were sitting with
their heads together next to the rabbit's box. The
man was an itinerant artist. They lived in a flimsy
dome—or at least they used to. He couldn't be doing
much more than barely keeping food on the table. Yet
his children were happy and healthy. And his wife
adored him, Charles acknowledged as he watched
Marilyn smile and lean her head against Joe's shoulder.

As much as it galled him to admit it, Charles knew
that this long-haired leftover from the hippie generation had found the secret to happiness that Charles
had yet to discover.

But he would, he vowed with renewed determination. If he had to study and dissect and mimic Joe Walker's every move, he would do it. He would make peace with his children, and make Judith love him again.

If someone like Joe Walker could do it, so could he.

Chapter Nine

"You can't see the car anymore," Alex announced. He looked at his parents, meeting first his mother's worried gaze and then his father's. "It's just a big white lump."

Jennifer crossed to the window and stood beside him. "I wish the phones were working."

"Why, so you can call Clarisse to gab?" he quipped. "A lot of good that would do us." But he nudged her shoulder gently with his elbow, and she responded with a wry grin.

"I guess being best friends with the mayor's daughter is no help at all in a blizzard."

Alex considered that. "I suppose her father

could call out the National Guard to come and rescue us."

"You want to leave?" Josie asked as she insinuated herself between the two Montgomery children. "This is so much fun. Why do you want to leave?"

Alex reached down and picked her up, flipping her over onto his back while she squealed in delight. "We don't want to leave, Josie. But it is kinda weird being stuck here with no electricity or telephones."

The child leaned forward and put her hands over his eyes. "You can't see anyway, so it doesn't matter."

"Oh, yeah?" He bounced her up and down. "What if Santa can't see to get here? What if the blizzard stops him?"

The little girl's humor fled. "Santa can always find his way, can't he?"

Alex could have bitten his tongue. Why had he said that? " 'Course he'll find us, Josie. Can't you take a joke?" He stared meaningfully at Jennifer.

"Oh. Yeah. That's right," Jennifer agreed. "Santa always finds his way. Don't you remember about Rudolph?"

"What's the matter, Josie? Afraid you won't have any presents on Christmas morning?" Robbie teased as he joined them at the window.

Josie gave her brother a relieved smile. Then she laughed. "No. I knew Santa would find us all along." Then, with the reckless courage of the well-loved child, she plunged off Alex's shoulders into the waiting arms of her brother. Once Robbie had her, he promptly began to tickle her.

"Stop it. Stop!" she shrieked amid her giggles.

"Okay. I'll stop. I'll tickle Jennifer instead!"

In a moment they were a mass of laughing, flailing

kids as Lucy also joined in. Tickling feet, underarms, waists, and necks, they collapsed in a pile. As the biggest, Alex had the advantage. But the others quickly figured that out and ganged up on him, until he was held down on the floor with Josie sitting on his chest.

"You've been a very bad boy," she said in a mock serious voice. But she couldn't keep the sparkle out of her blue eyes, and Alex grinned back up at her. "I don't know if Santa is going to bring you anything at all this year."

"He'll give him coal and switches." Lucy laughed, holding tight to one of Alex's legs.

" 'Course, there's still time to be a good boy," Josie continued.

"I'll do anything. Anything," Alex pleaded in a wavering, falsetto voice.

"Make him chop all the wood." Robbie suggested.

"No, make him wash the dishes," Jennifer threw in.

Josie tapped one pudgy finger against her chin. "I have a better idea. Alex has to play some Christmas songs for us. Okay?" She looked down at him. "Okay?"

Alex met the little girl's stare with a mixture of emotions. Christmas carols with an electric guitar? How embarrassing, even if he didn't have an amp or electricity. Still, he couldn't quite force himself to deny her request. She was so cute. And she still believed in Santa Claus.

He nodded slowly. "Okay. But it'll have to be some easy ones, because I don't know how to play any Christmas carols. I'll do figure a few out."

"Okay." She clambered off his chest and promptly

pushed everyone else off Alex. "Move. C'mon, get off," she ordered. "Alex is gonna play us some Christmas songs. And everybody has to sing."

By the time darkness fell, the living room was rife with new smells and sounds. Charles looked around with an odd sense of contentment. The fire, constantly supplied with logs to maintain a hot bed of coals, kept the room warm. The light from the hearth, the two oil lamps, and several candles cast a golden light over all. Perhaps it would not do for reading, but for simply sitting and watching, for listening and occasionally conversing, Charles found it splendid.

The five children were gathered in one corner, working on some scheme or another, judging by their whispers and muffled giggles. Josie had attached herself almost possessively to Alex, and he did not seem to mind. In her high little girl's voice she sang snatches of Christmas songs to Alex as he worked out the chords for them.

Joe had given him the guitar he'd found earlier, and after a brief discussion, they had decided to use the strings from Alex's electric guitar to replace the ones on the old acoustic. Though less than ideal, under the circumstances, it would suffice.

Marilyn and Judith had a stew bubbling on the hearth and had promised more popcorn and hot chocolate to go with the caroling. All in all, it was as close to a scene from a Hallmark commercial as Charles had ever experienced, and he found it both sweet and inexplicably sad. This was how Christmas should be —every year and for everybody. This was exactly what he had wanted.

As if she had been thinking the very same thought,

Judith looked up. Their gazes caught and held. What Charles saw in her eyes was a mirror of his emotions, a sweet soft stirring of feelings that was nonetheless tinged with sorrow.

He swallowed hard, willing her to struggle past the sadness. Without thinking, he mouthed the words *I love you*. For a moment longer their eyes clung. Then she looked away.

Charles knew she'd been affected by his impulsive avowal, for her eyes had widened and she'd suddenly seemed more vulnerable than ever. He too was frightened by the emotions he felt. It was almost as if he'd never said the words before, or more accurately, never truly meant them. But he meant them now. More than he'd ever thought he could.

"Boy, are you guys gonna be surprised," Josie announced with a sage nod of her curly head.

Charles looked at the little girl, who had come up before him. "Oh, we are, are we?" On impulse he reached forward to stroke the golden haze of curls. "You know what, little angel baby? I bet you're right." He sat back in the chair, consumed with a rare feeling of well-being as he continued to smile at the five-year-old. "I can hardly wait to see what you hooligans have cooked up for us."

They ate dinner by firelight and candlelight amid the infectious good humor of the children. The adults, however, were not in much need of prompting by the young ones. Everyone seemed filled with good spirits. But then, it *was* the day before Christmas Eve, Charles thought with enormous contentment.

Judith sat to his left. As he finished the last spoonful of the hearty stew, he wiped his mouth. Then he placed one arm around Judith's shoulders and drew her nearer. When she looked around in surprise, he planted a kiss directly on her lips. "Thanks for a wonderful meal."

"Ooooh!" Lucy teased at once. "No kissing at the table until *everyone's* finished."

Charles laughed, more in the pleasure of the moment than at Lucy's joking. Kissing his wife had been wonderful; her lips were warm and she tasted of beef stew. And best of all, he'd made her blush. Her cheeks were clearly tinged with pink, even in the flickering light of the candles on the table. She looked young and incredibly beautiful like that.

He glanced over at Lucy. "Well. I certainly wish everyone would hurry up and finish so I can kiss her again."

Judith lowered her eyes in confusion. Jennifer, however, was not at a loss for words.

"Hey, you know what we need? We need mistletoe. You always have to have mistletoe at Christmastime."

"All right, Jenn," Alex said. " 'Fess up. Who do you want to kiss anyway?"

"Me? I don't want to kiss anyone," she exclaimed. But she couldn't prevent a guilty glance at Robbie.

"Yeah," Lucy jumped in. "Moms and Dads don't need mistletoe to kiss. So *you* must want to kiss somebody!"

Into all this raucous good humor Josie piped up eagerly, "I want to kiss Alex." She rose on the chair from her knees to stand upright. She waved her fork around to get attention. "I want to kiss Alex! He's my boyfriend."

Charles watched Alex get up too, then pick up Josie and spin her around in his arms. But it wasn't the Alex he'd known for the past few years. This was a different Alex, a gentle, considerate boy who planted a kiss on the little girl's cheek.

"Okay, girlfriend, I kissed you. Now you kiss me."

The other children whistled and hooted as Josie gave him a long, loud smack on his cheek. Then everyone started clapping.

"See," Alex said as he put her down on her chair. "You don't need mistletoe for an excuse to kiss somebody." He grinned at everyone, and it was as if a contagion were set loose upon them all. Joe kissed Lucy; Marilyn kissed Robbie. Charles took that opportunity to kiss Judith again. With an embarrassed laugh Judith reached out for Jennifer.

"Come here. Remember when we used to give you sandwich kisses?" She pressed a kiss to the girl's left cheek while Charles immediately pressed one to the other side of Jennifer's laughing face.

Again Charles's gaze met Judith's in the old familiar way. They needed to talk, he decided as her blue eyes held with his. While these warm feelings enveloped them all, they needed to talk about their relationship. Maybe later that night.

He smiled at Judith as Jennifer broke away laughing, and rejoiced inside when she smiled back.

Alex tossed Josie up in the air, making her squeal with delight. Then he kissed her again and planted her back on her chair. "See what you started, Josie?" he teased.

"*I* didn't start it. Jennifer did," the child replied, pointing at Jennifer.

"*I* didn't start it," Jennifer protested in turn. "It's all Dad's fault."

"*Moi?*" Charles said, feigning innocence. "All I did

was kiss my wife." He leaned over and kissed Judith once more, taking a secret pleasure in the color that rose in her face. "A man does have *some* rights."

Amid the continuing good humor and boisterous jesting, the meal was completed and the cleanup began. Marilyn marshaled the children's aid and sent Judith and Charles to sit by the fire with the firm admonition to relax and do "whatever."

As he guided Judith to the big couch, Charles could not have been more jubilant. He was definitely making headway. Never in his wildest dreams could he have thought a blizzard and the constant presence of a quintet of strangers—very strange strangers at that—would lend itself to a truly merry Christmas. Yet that was precisely what was happening. His children were behaving; his wife had let him kiss her— not once but three times—and blushed at his attentions. He was happy, so happy he felt he would burst with the magnitude of it. Things were going to work out. He was sure of it.

But as he sank down into the thick-cushioned sofa, Judith disengaged his hand from her shoulder. She took a step back, glancing only briefly at him before averting her gaze. "The rabbit . . . someone should check on it."

"One of the kids can do that, Jude. Come on. Sit down with me for a little while."

"Well . . . I will. I will. Just as soon as I do a couple of things."

She backed away before he could stop her, and just as fast as hope had buoyed him up, so now did despair let him down with a hard thump. He watched her fuss over the rabbit in its box in the corner. He saw Josie come to join her and the way Judith's hand gently stroked the child's curly head.

She could be so kind, he thought as yearning stabbed painfully through him. So gentle and loving and giving of herself. She'd been that way with him for as long as he'd known her—all his life, he realized. He could barely remember a life before Judith.

But she didn't want to be that way with him anymore. Anguish threatened to overwhelm him, but he fought it down. He would never win her back by giving up. He never gave up. That's what had gotten him where he was today. He never gave up, and he would not give up now.

His gaze sharpened on Judith, taking in the familiar shape of her, the familiar profile, and soft shine of her hair. He knew her so well. At least he'd always thought he did. It was clear, however, that there were facets of her he'd never learned.

But he was willing to learn them now, so why wouldn't she let him? If only she would try a little. If only she would bend. It wouldn't take much to bring them back to how they were before.

If only he could get her away from that group of meddlesome women she'd been meeting with. He sighed, knowing he couldn't come right out and demand she quit her roundtable. If only he could distract her from them, find some other way to keep her busy.

His skin prickled and he looked up to see Joe's eyes focused on him. Marilyn moved into her husband's embrace at that very moment; her gaze, too, turned toward Charles.

For a scant moment he had the oddest feeling that they knew what he was thinking. And that they somehow disapproved. But he shook off the feeling as foolish. Besides, they of all people should approve of his efforts to keep his family together. Still, their steady gazes left him unsettled, and he struggled for a way to get back the warm camaraderie he'd felt during the meal.

"How about . . . how about those carols? Is every-one nearly ready to sing them now? How about you, Josie?" He crossed to the little girl and crouched down before her. He gave her a determined smile. "Are you ready for Christmas caroling?"

The smile he received back from the cherub-faced child was like a beam of sunshine. It warmed him through and through, and he was tempted to pick her up and hug her tight. But before he could act on that impulse, she turned away.

"C'mon, Alex!" she called as she ran toward the boy. "Let's do our songs now."

Alex caught her as she jumped for him, then tucked her under one arm, carrying her like a limp rag. "Sack of potatoes," he cried as he paraded through the room. "Sack of potatoes."

Jennifer at once swatted Josie's upended rump, echoing "sack of potatoes." Lucy and Robbie quickly caught on, and in a moment Josie was squealing with laughter. When Alex finally put her down, she promptly whacked him on his rear end, shouting, "Sack of potatoes."

"Aw, you got me," he laughed. Then, spying her flushed features, he pressed a hand to her brow.

"Has her fever come back?" Marilyn asked at once.

"I don't think so," Alex answered. "What do you think?"

"I'm *not* sick," Josie protested as her mother felt her brow.

"No, I don't think you are," her mother agreed with a relieved smile at Alex. "She's just pink from being upside down."

"Oh, man, I'm sorry. I didn't know."

"No, no. It's fine. She's fine. Now, shall we sing those songs you've been working on?"

As the children huddled, finalizing the details of their performance, Charles could not help but stare at Alex in amazement. His concern for Josie was so unexpected. So unlike him. Charles glanced at Judith and caught the same puzzled expression on her face. As if she felt his gaze, she met his eyes, and he knew they shared the same thought. This child of theirs— this boy struggling to become a man—had sides to him they did not know.

For a moment her face softened and he felt the smile in her eyes before she looked back at the knot of children. He did not know as much as he'd thought about her, he decided once again. Nor did he really know his son.

He swallowed hard at that admission, then focused on Jennifer. Was she, too, more than just the silly twelve-year-old he saw? He watched as she smoothed Josie's hair back and tucked her shirt in. Then she lined everyone up, tallest to shortest, shushing Josie's demand to be next to Alex.

"You can stand next to him in a minute, okay? Just wait."

She was just like her mother, he realized, a born organizer, although Judith was more low-key about it. Jennifer seemed to combine his own brash style with her mother's need for order, and that was good.

But just like Judith, she needed more from him than she was getting. If he didn't want to end up as distanced from her as he was from her mother and brother, he needed to pay more attention to her needs.

"Okay, we're ready," Jennifer announced. She glanced nervously down the line of children, trying to restrain a giggle. "We each picked out a special song. One we like the best. But everybody has to sing along." Her eyes danced in anticipation as she stared at her parents. "We're starting with the youngest first."

"That's me!" Josie broke in, jumping up and down. "Can I start now?"

"Yeah, go on," Lucy said, giving her a little shove forward.

The children all sat down in a circle, with Alex on a footstool with the guitar. Josie stood next to him with one hand on his knee. She waited expectantly as he strummed the opening chords, then, with her eyes fixed on him, began to sing "Away in a Manger."

The other kids joined in with her almost at once, as did the adults. Joe's voice was deep and mellow; Marilyn's a sweet soprano. Though Charles's voice was hesitant at first, he slowly gained confidence.

Judith, however, found it impossible to sing. At the first strains of the song a sudden rush of emotions had caught her unawares, and now her throat filled with them. How like an angel Josie appeared with her sweet baby voice raised in song. How angelic all of them looked. Even Alex, with his shaggy hair, protruding Adam's apple, and gangly arms and legs, was a vision of all God intended in His children.

She took a quick breath, willing away the tears

that threatened. How blessed she was to have them both. How truly blessed. Then Charles nudged her. "Aren't you going to sing?" he whispered as Josie began the same verse a second time.

Judith blinked and managed a nod, then began to mouth the words, still afraid to trust her voice. In many ways she had been blessed with Charles also. When he was with her—really with her, heart and soul—no woman could want for more. But he was so seldom with her that way anymore.

But when he'd kissed her at the table earlier, she had felt, at least for a short while, like he was with her. She'd been caught off guard by the warmth of his sweetly intimate gesture, and for a moment she'd felt all the old feelings. The deep emotional ones, as well as the stirring physical ones. At that moment she'd wanted to hold him close forever. And yet she knew better than to fall into that same old trap—that simple solution that was no solution at all. It was only nostalgia getting to her once again.

Still, the crestfallen expression on his face when she'd refused to sit on the couch with him had cut her to the heart. And now, with everything so perfect, with the children singing Christmas carols and all the rest . . . If only it could be like this forever.

"That was good. Real good," Jennifer said. Her cheeks were rosy and flushed. "Okay, you're next, Lucy."

Lucy stepped up, pressing her lips together self-consciously. She grinned at her parents. "I picked 'O Holy Night,' because it's my very favorite."

Judith was able to sing this one, but she still had to guard against the constant threat of tears. There was something so emotional about it all, even in the middle of their gaiety. Jennifer and Robbie sat side by side, singing quite earnestly. Josie was draped over Alex's back, her face on his shoulder, right next to his. He glanced frequently at the guitar as he sang, but at one point he caught his mother's eye and grinned, and he was once more her little boy.

Jennifer, too, would always be her baby, she decided when the girl rose to lead the next song. They all sang her choice, "White Christmas," with considerable gusto and laughter, and when it was done, Judith felt more in control of herself. This was truly a perfect way to celebrate Christmas. Even Charles seemed to be enjoying himself enormously, despite the blow she'd dealt him earlier.

"Your turn now, Robbie. Go on," Josie ordered. She grabbed his hand and yanked at him until, with many embarrassed glances, he got up.

"I told them I didn't want to do one," he said, his face sheepish. "I don't sing too good."

"Oh, yes you do," Marilyn countered. "I hear you in the shower sometimes."

"Aw, Mom," he complained when everyone laughed. Finally he sighed and straightened up with many a baleful glare at the three giggling girls. Only when Alex strummed the opening chords of the song, grinning encouragingly at him, did the boy settle down.

"Okay, okay. The song I picked . . ." He paused and a devious little grin lit his face. "The song I picked is 'Grandma Got Run Over by a Reindeer.' " His grin grew when everyone laughed. Then he glanced at Alex. "Are you ready?"

"Ready." Alex began the introduction again, and once Robbie started singing, his case of stage fright seemed to disappear. Not everyone knew all the words, and there was as much giggling as there was singing. But eventually they got through it, cheering Robbie as he took his final bows.

Then it was Alex's turn, and Judith found herself avidly contemplating his choice. He cleared his throat when Robbie sat down, and concentrated on the guitar, fiddling with it and adjusting the tuning keys until Josie leaned her full weight against his back.

"C'mon, Alex. You can do it."

He laughed, lifting his head at last. "Okay, here we go. I picked 'Silent Night,' but it's a little different than usual." He paused. "It would sound better on an electric guitar, but . . . I'll do the best I can."

Judith glanced at Charles, and received back a look as puzzled as her own. She couldn't imagine what Alex had in mind.

The song began as usual. Alex's guitar work was clear and pure, chords at first, then gradually in the second verse progressing to more and more finger work. When they finished singing the second verse, however, he continued to play. It was an odd, very contemporary rendition of the traditional song, and as his fingers flew over the strings, Judith knew she'd never been so proud of him. Unconsciously, her hand moved to grasp Charles's arm, and when the song was done she was once more close to tears.

Everyone clapped and Alex blushed and ducked his head once more. Then Charles leaned forward.

"You know what that reminds me of? Jimi Hendrix did a version of 'The Star-Spangled Banner' back in the sixties or seventies."

Alex stared at his father in surprise. "I know.

That's what I was thinking about when I wrote this version of 'Silent Night.' But it would be a lot better on the electric guitar with some tremolo, distortion, and a wah-wah pedal."

"Nobody liked the Hendrix version when it came out," Joe remarked. "At least, not too many regular folks."

Alex shrugged. "So?" He stared at Joe measuringly. "I don't care if people don't like what I write and play. That is, I *hope* they'll like it. But even if they don't, I'm still gonna play what I want to play."

The man grinned at Alex and then at Judith and Charles. "I fear you've got a true artist on your hands here. More power to him, I say."

Alex grinned, too. Then his gaze slid to his father. "Did you like Jimi Hendrix when you were young?"

Judith tensed as Charles considered his reply. *Please don't say the wrong thing,* she prayed.

It must have been a magical night, she was later to think. The spirit of goodwill had infected them all, even Charles, for he had answered his son with a self-deprecating chuckle.

"At first I thought his 'Star-Spangled Banner' was an insult. You know, unpatriotic. But . . . well, it grew on me. I guess just because it was different didn't mean it was an insult to our country."

Alex had met his father's eyes a long moment after that, and Judith had felt a leap of joy in her heart.

Eventually the singing resumed, sometimes with guitar accompaniment, and sometimes without, depending on Alex's ability to easily pick up the key of the songs everyone suggested. But despite missed chords, forgotten words, and the occasional off-key note, Judith thought it the most wonderful music she'd ever heard.

The heavenly hosts could never have sung so sweetly.

Chapter **Ten**

Sleeping in a room with one's own children was not in the least conducive to marital intimacy. Charles lay beside Judith on the spacious bed staring up at the faint shadows flickering on the beams that supported the cathedral ceiling and listened to the faint breathing of Alex and Jennifer. They had dragged mattresses into the master bedroom from one of the other bedrooms, and lit the fireplace. Though the room was not toasty, it was bearable. The Walkers had slept on couches and chairs downstairs.

At least *they* had no privacy either, Charles thought with sour satisfaction. Then he sighed and

shifted so that his hip rested against Judith's back.
Truth was, his children, the storm, and the Walkers'
presence were only excuses. He had no idea how
Judith would have reacted to any amorous attempts
on his part. It was probably best not to know, either,
for he wasn't sure he could bear it if she had turned
away.

He twisted his head to stare at the glowing logs in
the fireplace, and replayed the day in his mind. From
the worst of beginnings, it had somehow progressed
into one of the most memorable evenings of his life.
The warmth and happiness he'd felt while they'd
sung Christmas carols were unlike anything he'd
ever felt. The closest thing he could compare it to was
the birth of his children. That overwhelming sense of
well-being. He smiled, remembering.

Later they'd played charades, laughing, shouting,
and one by one making fools of themselves. He'd
thought he would never get them to guess the title
Marilyn had given him. *All I Really Need to Know I
Learned in Kindergarten.* It had been a real killer,
but he'd done it.

Judith had enjoyed the evening just as much as he
had. She'd laughed and teased, and the lines of tension he'd noticed in her face recently had not been so
evident. It had been just like old times, and that very
fact was what reassured him now that those times
could be recaptured once more.

Still, the thought of her rebuff terrified him.

Outside the wind blew, battering against the windows. The storm showed no sign of abating. If anything, it seemed even more violent than before. It
was a good thing they'd already cut down the Christ-

mas tree. By tomorrow they might not even be able to get out of the house.

Once more he smiled. Actually, that wasn't proving to be as terrible a situation as he might have thought.

Charles awoke with a start. He was disoriented at first, for the room was dark and he knew the bed was not his own. But then he heard the sound of someone moving about, and when he lifted his head and spied Alex, everything came back to him. The house. The Walkers. The storm.

Alex must have sensed his father's eyes on him, for he looked up and met Charles's gaze. Neither of them spoke; Judith and Jennifer were still asleep. But Charles couldn't help wondering why Alex was up. Despite the dim light, he sensed it was morning— just past dawn. That was hardly an hour Alex was familiar with. What had roused such a late sleeper as Alex?

As easily as he could, he rose from the bed, taking care not to disturb Judith. She was burrowed down into the pillows and feather comforter, hiding from the chill in the air. While Charles donned slippers and a robe, he watched Alex carefully feed several heavy logs into the fire. Shivering, he crossed to stand before the hearth, holding his robe open to collect the heat.

"Too cold to sleep?" he whispered to Alex.

Alex shrugged. "Not really. I don't know. I was just lying there so . . . I thought I might as well make myself useful."

They both stared into the fire, watching as the embers glowed hotter, then slowly broke into small licking flames around the fresh logs.

"If I'd known you could chop wood so well, I wouldn't have bothered buying firewood for the house these past few winters."

Alex shrugged again. "I guess it wouldn't be so much fun if I had to do it all the time."

"No," Charles agreed. "I guess not." He closed the robe and belted it, much warmed by the heated silk lining.

Alex continued to poke at the embers, stirring them until the bottom log caught. In a matter of seconds the fire began to grow, casting its warm light over the rest of the room. Charles looked around the bedroom, at the chaos of extra mattresses, piled-up covers, and discarded shoes. It was strange how satisfying it was.

"It's sort of like summer camp," Alex commented.

Charles looked back at his son. "Is that right? I never went to a summer camp. But I always wondered. Now I know."

"Well, it's not exactly like this. There's always at least one jerk in your cabin. And the counselors can sometimes be a real pain."

Charles let out a soft chuckle. "I'm afraid that could be said of life in general. There's always a jerk in every crowd. And someone's always being a pain in the ass. In the neck," he amended.

Alex grinned at that, and for a moment father and son basked in the easy banter between them. Charles sat down on the hearth and rubbed his arms as he stifled a yawn.

"You think between the two of us we could manage to go downstairs and start a pot of coffee?"

Alex nodded and stood up. "It didn't look too hard. I can get the water going. You can figure out the coffeepot."

The coffee turned out way too strong. Charles had to cut it half and half with milk. But in the quiet of the slowly lightening living room, he decided it was one of the best cups of coffee he'd ever had. Though he and Alex didn't talk much, there was a peace between them that was as rare as it was wonderful. Alex carved on the wood chip Robbie had given him while Charles just sipped his coffee and enjoyed the fire.

Rogers had done him a great favor when he'd lent him this place, Charles thought, smiling to himself. He'd have to do the man a good turn. Maybe he wouldn't shift his construction loan to First Federal. Then he shook his head at such a perverse thought. Boy, was he getting maudlin! Points and interest were all that mattered in financing a project like his. Not emotions.

Still, he might look into doing some sort of resort-type development. Rogers might be interested in working with him on that.

"Say, Alex. How would you feel about us having a place like this all our own?"

The boy looked up. "That would be cool. Are you gonna buy one? How about this one?"

"I was thinking more on the lines of developing a small resort area. You know, a cluster of homes with a few community amenities. A health club. Stores. That sort of thing."

When Alex didn't look away in disinterest, Charles could hardly believe it. The boy had never evidenced the slightest curiosity about his work. It was one of the things that had always aggravated Charles. But now all that was changing.

"Yeah, I think it would be a nice switch, building something out in the woods instead of in town." He paused. "Maybe you could take a few trips to the site with me as it was being built."

"That would be cool," Alex repeated. "But how expensive would the houses be?"

Charles shrugged, too elated by his sudden success with Alex to care about anything else. "Oh, I don't know. We could go as high as the market could bear. Starting, say, at two hundred thousand and topping out at three or four."

A slight frown creased Alex's brow and he looked down at his carving. "So people like the Walkers couldn't afford to live there."

"Well, no. No, I guess not." Charles glanced at the people still asleep on the sofa sleeper, then lowered his voice and leaned forward. "But they aren't the kind of people in the market for second homes at any price, Alex. Resort developments like I'm talking about are for the fairly well off—"

"Like us," the boy interrupted. He raised his eyes and at once Charles knew he'd lost him. For a fleeting few minutes they'd been on the same track, but not anymore. If only he could make him understand.

"Look, Alex. You can't deny reality," he whispered anxiously. "Some people make more money than others. Those are the ones who shop in high-class shopping centers. The ones who stay in hotels. The ones who buy vacation homes. That's not necessarily a bad thing."

Alex concentrated on the piece of wood in his hand, refusing to look at his father. "No. I guess not."

The silence that followed was not like the previous one. The old strain was back, only now it was worse than ever, for Charles was aware, as he'd never been, of what he was missing.

When Joe and Marilyn roused a few minutes later, he was not sure whether to be relieved or annoyed. At least they filled the awkward gap between him and Alex. But the very sight of Joe Walker sitting next to Alex, giving him pointers about his carving, was enough to raise Charles's blood pressure.

That's my son, he wanted to cry. *Mine!* But he couldn't do that and he knew it, so instead he went into the chilly half bath to wash up.

When he came out, Judith was downstairs, sitting near the fire. Josie was up too, sitting on her father's lap, next to Alex, while Jennifer and Lucy were apparently both still asleep. Marilyn had poured herself a cup of coffee, and at the first sip her nose automatically wrinkled in surprise.

"It's a little too strong. I know," Charles muttered.

"No. No, it's fine," she insisted. "I'll just add more milk. Judith, are you ready for a cup? How about you, Joe?"

If it hadn't been for his failure with Alex, Charles would have thought the morning as pleasant a one as he'd ever passed. He hardly even missed having contact with his office. After all, the business was half Doug's. He could handle anything that came up.

They worked on the puzzle. They played games. They read and ate and drew pictures. It was odd, almost as if there were no distinction between adults and children. They all played and teased and had fun on the same level.

But there was a sense of unreality about it, and

every once in a while, Charles would pause and stare about him. He couldn't quite immerse himself entirely in the moment. Judith appeared completely relaxed and at ease, and Jennifer and Alex were both having a wonderful time. Not once had they argued with each other. The teasing, which normally would have deteriorated into shouts and tears, today remained only that, good-natured teasing and laughter.

But Charles was unable to let himself go that much. He kept studying Joe Walker, looking for the clue that would allow him to relate to Alex in the same way Joe did to Robbie. He needed to learn how to make Judith laugh and react the way Marilyn did when Joe whispered in her ear or simply touched her arm.

Try as he might, however, he felt as if he were only scratching the surface. Though he spoke to his children, and chatted with Judith over the puzzle, he had the distinct feeling it was going nowhere. He was reminded uncomfortably of situations at work with employees who had heard what he said but insisted on doing as they pleased. He'd always ended up firing them.

"Say, boys, how about bringing in more wood?" Judith asked. She was standing before the window, gazing out into a mysterious white world. "The snow has stopped, but it's so deep I can't imagine the utility companies getting out this far anytime soon."

"You mean we're stuck here for Christmas?" Josie asked, a huge grin on her little face.

"I think so," her father answered.

"Yippie!" She bounded over to Alex, but stopped

short of leaping into his arms because he was carving again. "We're stuck here! We're stuck here!"

While the children all celebrated their grand adventure, Charles noticed a solemn look pass between Marilyn and Joe. Only Judith seemed unperturbed by the situation.

Was it that she was relieved that the Walkers would have to stay—that she would not have to be left alone with her own family? With her own husband? The very thought tightened a knot in Charles's stomach.

Judith did indeed find it hard to be upset with their snowbound situation. But it was not that she didn't want to be alone with her family. It was rather that she wanted more of the warm feelings the Walkers helped to create within her family. The peace. If this was to be their last Christmas as a whole family unit, then she wanted it to be good. And if it needed the Walkers to be good, then so be it.

"Marilyn, could we talk?" she asked when everyone else was preoccupied. The boys had gone outside for wood. Charles appeared to be reading. Joe and the girls were checking on Roger Rabbit. "We need to plan for tonight."

"For tonight?" Marilyn asked as they stood near the curtained-off stairwell.

"It's Christmas Eve. Santa has to find us."

Marilyn sighed, understanding now what she meant. "Don't worry. Robbie knows and so does Lucy."

"Josie still believes in Santa Claus."

Marilyn looked across the room at her youngest. "Yes, she does. I guess I'll just tell her that Santa decided to leave everything at her own house."

"You don't have to do that."

Marilyn smiled. "I think I know what you have in mind, Judith. And I appreciate it. But I don't think that's necessary."

"Actually . . ." Judith paused, fumbling with words that did not come easily. "Actually, you couldn't be more wrong. My children have . . . well, they have a lot. But I'm not sure they've ever developed a sense of responsibility for others. Please, don't deprive them of this opportunity," she implored.

Their eyes met in complete understanding. Finally Marilyn laughed. "Who's the salesman in your family, anyway? You make it awfully hard to turn down your offer."

"Then don't turn it down. Alex and Jennifer have a closet full of gifts upstairs. They won't miss a few."

"Are you going to let them decide which gifts to share?"

Judith bit her lip in indecision. "I'm not sure if I should make the choices, or they should."

"Why not ask them? Let them decide?"

Judith caught Alex as he came in with wood. She corralled Jennifer as well, and in the icy kitchen they huddled.

"Josie still believes in Santa Claus," she began without preamble. "Unless you agree to share your gifts with the Walker children, she'll know it's all make-believe." Then she waited.

Alex and Jennifer glanced at each other. "Did you get us anything a little girl like her would like?" Alex asked.

"Well, not much," Judith admitted. "But I want to do more than just share with Josie. I want to make sure *everyone* has a happy Christmas morning."

Alex shrugged. "Sure. No problem."

Jennifer stared at Alex in disbelief. "You mean share my stuff with *all* of them? But there won't be anything left for *me*."

"Get real, Jenn," Alex scoffed. "You're not exactly what anyone would call deprived. What's your problem?"

Judith looked at her daughter. The war going on inside the girl was clear from the look on her face. This was Jennifer who loved her name-brand clothes and jewelry—who could live in the shopping malls her father built. Asking her to give up even one of the elegantly wrapped boxes she'd seen unloaded from the car was asking a lot.

Jennifer sighed. "They've probably never gotten as much stuff for Christmas as we get, have they?" she asked as she shifted from one foot to the other. Then she slowly grinned at her mother, and Judith let out the breath she'd unconsciously been holding. "Okay, Mom. Go ahead and divide up the gifts. Just don't ask *me* to choose which ones to keep and which ones to give away," she added ruefully.

Alex laughed out loud and threw one arm around his little sister. "It'll only hurt for a little while, Jenn. I'm sure Mom will make it up to you the next time you both go shopping."

Jennifer laughed, too. "Hey, you're right! If I'm smart, I can milk this for lots of good stuff."

Judith was caught off guard by the quick flood of love that overwhelmed her. Tears stung her eyes and she couldn't trust herself to speak. Instead, she drew her two children to her in a tight, emotional embrace.

"I love you both so much," she whispered in a voice that shook.

When they broke apart, she could see that they were as affected as she was. Alex swallowed hard and looked sheepish, while Jennifer brushed away her own tears.

"This is going to be a great Christmas, Mom. Just like Dad promised."

"Yes." Judith nodded and pressed her lips together. "Just like he promised."

But once Christmas was over, what then?

Judith had disappeared upstairs with Marilyn some time ago. Charles couldn't help peering at the curtained-off stairwell one more time. They must be freezing up there. No doubt they were planning for tonight. For Christmas Eve and Christmas morning.

"Lucy! Something's wrong. Quick! Come see!"

Charles glanced up at Jennifer's fearful tone. She was leaning over the rabbit's box, but when Lucy rushed over, she looked up.

"Roger Rabbit doesn't look good. I think she's—" She broke off abruptly, her face reflecting her sudden panic.

"Dad. Dad!" Lucy instinctively yelled for her parent.

"What's wrong, girls?" Charles said, hurrying over to them.

Robbie came in from the kitchen. "Dad's in the basement, Lucy. What do you want him for?"

"Roger Rabbit! She's—I don't know—she's shaking. And . . . and . . . Oh, Robbie, I think she's gonna die!"

"Dad!" Robbie bellowed at once. "Dad!" Then he scrambled across the room to join the worried group.

"Let me take a look," Charles said.

He put a hand on Jennifer's shoulder and she looked up at him. "I don't think you should do anything, Dad. Just wait for Joe."

Their eyes met for a long moment. Charles saw the worry in his daughter's eyes and he squeezed her shoulder. "Maybe I can do something," he said encouragingly.

She swallowed and shook her head. "This is too important, Dad. We'd better wait for Joe—"

She broke off as Joe, Alex, and Josie hurried into the room. Charles felt a cold rush of air that might have come with them from the unheated kitchen and basement. But the chill he felt was rooted deeper than that.

This was too important, Jennifer had said. Too important for him to deal with. She'd rather wait for Joe Walker.

Charles stepped back as the others crowded forward. Josie was in Alex's arms. As she began to cry, Alex pressed her face to his shoulder and tried to comfort her. Lucy and Jennifer knelt to one side with Robbie between them. The boy put an arm around each of them, and the three clung together, giving and seeking comfort as Joe examined the animal.

Charles knew what the outcome would be. He'd seen the rabbit's convulsions, and knew it was in the final throes of its death. No one could change that, not even the almighty Joe Walker. Jennifer would see. The man was only human. Just like him.

Yet as Charles watched the distraught children, he suddenly wished Joe *could* change the inevitable. He wished the man could save the rabbit, even if it confirmed Jennifer's and Alex's exalted opinion of him. Anything to erase the stricken expressions from their faces.

When Joe's head drooped in defeat, Charles knew it was over. For an instant the men's eyes met, and they shared a moment of complete understanding. No matter how much they each wanted for their children—for their children's happiness—there were things that would always be beyond their ability to provide. One rabbit's life seemed on the surface a very small thing. But somehow it mattered very much.

At that moment Marilyn and Judith came down the stairs, their cheeks and noses rosy from the frozen reaches of the upper floor.

"—thaw out the turkey," Judith was saying. But she stopped when she spied the miserable group huddled around the rabbit's box. "What's wrong?"

"Joe?" Marilyn scurried down the last three steps. "What happened? Is the rabbit . . ." Her question trailed off as she met her husband's gaze.

"Mama!" Josie cried.

Alex crossed to Marilyn and handed her the crying child. "Roger's dead," he said.

Charles heard the quiver in his son's voice and knew how hard Alex fought to control his own emotions. Charles suddenly remembered every time he'd told his son that big boys didn't cry, and he regretted it. He felt like crying himself, though not because of the rabbit's death. It was Jennifer's words that made him want to cry. It was her innocent observation that her father could not help—not when it was truly important. He could build high-rise hotels and extravagant shopping malls. He could provide his family with the best of everything—houses, clothes, cars. But he couldn't provide his own little girl with the emotional comfort she wanted. She would pick a complete stranger over him.

Tears blurred his vision, though he sternly fought them down. He watched as Judith and Marilyn gathered their children to them. He saw Joe wrap the still rabbit in a towel and lay it back in its box. Only when Joe took the box to the kitchen did Charles move from his position apart from the others.

"Don't cry," he murmured to Jennifer, who had her head buried in her mother's shoulder. He touched the tangled blond hair, then extended his arm to encircle both girl and mother. Without thinking, he also encircled Alex's shoulder so that they stood together, all four of them. He sought out Judith's eyes and was gratified beyond all understanding to see the need in them. She needed him!

He bent his head until their foreheads met and then he just stood there, connected to her once more. Connected to them all.

It was Alex who pulled back first. His young face was composed again, and Charles found himself marveling at the mixture of boy and man so evident: the first hint of the beard to come—peach fuzz; the faint remnants of acne on his chin; the need to be manly when he wanted to cry like a little boy.

Jennifer's face was wet with undisguised tears when she straightened up. "If we could have gotten her to the vet, she would have lived."

"Maybe. Maybe not," Judith replied with a sad smile. "Some things are beyond our control, honey. Sometimes, no matter how much we want something —no matter how hard we try—it can never be. All you can do is accept it and go on."

Her gaze met Charles's, and all at once his sense of connectedness vanished. Was she talking about the rabbit's death or their marriage? He tried to read her face, but she was looking at Jennifer now, smoothing the girl's hair back and wiping the tears from her face. What had she meant?

Charles cleared his throat, desperate to get hold of a situation that seemed to be spiraling out of his control. "I know this has upset everybody," he said. "If you like, after we get out of here, I'll buy you another pet rabbit. All of you," he amended, including the Walker children in his sweeping gaze.

Marilyn gave him a faint smile. "That's very kind, but—"

"I don't *want* another rabbit," Josie broke in plaintively. "I only want Roger."

"Hush, now, sweetheart," her mother said. "Roger has gone up to heaven. You remember how we talked about that before?"

The little girl reluctantly nodded, then buried her head against her mother's neck again. "But I want her here," she sobbed.

"I'll get you another rabbit," Charles ventured, trying to placate the child. "You'll be able to play with it and everything."

Marilyn shook her head. "If Roger had recovered, eventually we would have let her go. She was a wild creature. The children know they're not allowed to keep wild creatures as pets unless they can't fend for themselves anymore."

"That makes sense." Judith squeezed Jennifer's shoulder before the girl could object. "A rabbit isn't like a dog or a cat. You'd probably have to keep it in a cage all the time. What kind of life would that be for the poor animal?"

Jennifer finally agreed, as did the other children. But as they slowly dispersed back to their various activities, Charles felt doubly devastated. Could he do nothing right? Once again he had somehow screwed up. All he'd wanted was to make them happy. Was offering to buy them a pet rabbit so awful?

Yet Charles knew it was not the idea of a pet rabbit that was the problem. Judith and Marilyn—even Joe —provided a comfort to their children that he was simply unable to. They offered solace; he offered to buy something.

He turned and made his way blindly to the chair he'd occupied before. But though he picked up the book again, he did not read. Instead his eyes followed Judith.

Was that what he did to her, too? Offered her the things money could buy but not what her heart truly craved? He wanted to cry out in frustration. What was it she wanted? If he knew, he would get it for her. He would do it for her. But he didn't know what it was. He didn't have a clue.

He watched as she removed the turkey from its plastic bag and set it in a large pan. He stared as she washed her hands in a bucket of water kept luke-warm by its proximity to the fire. And all the while his emotions veered from desolation to fury, from helpless love to something very close to hatred. She had no right to abandon him now. She had no right to undermine him this way. He deserved better than that.

Judith laughed softly at something Marilyn said, then murmured a reply. When she glanced up and met Charles's gaze, however, her smile faded. She looked away and Charles knew he must have been scowling. Glaring even. But he couldn't help it. Dammit, what did she expect from him?

"We need to bury her." Lucy stood before her father with Jennifer next to her. "We need to say prayers over her to make sure she gets to heaven right away."

"We'll have to wait for better weather," Joe said. "It's way too nasty outside now, honey. Besides, the ground is probably frozen."

"Well." Lucy looked at Jennifer for ideas.

"We could at least have a memorial service. You know, so her soul can go on up to heaven even if her body's still down here," Jennifer said. "I think it would make Josie feel better," she added in a hushed tone.

Joe smiled then, and even Charles couldn't help but thaw out inside as well. Jennifer was not usually so concerned with other people's feelings—unless it was a boy she thought was "cute." He wondered what kind of big sister she might have made. But that automatically made him think of Judith, and he stole another glance at her.

Jennifer would never be a big sister. The way things were going, she might very well end up being one of those Saturday children—with her father just one day a week, and her mother the rest of the time.

Or perhaps the other way around, he thought vindictively. Why should he give up his children just because Judith was being irrational?

Yet even as he watched, Jennifer ran over to her mother. The two blond heads bent together as the girl whispered in Judith's ear, and Charles knew at once that he could never fight Judith for custody of their children. He could never be so cruel to her.

Why was it so easy for her to be cruel to him?

"Please take Roger Rabbit up to heaven," Josie began the ceremony. Her hands were clasped together and she looked like a little angel. If God was listening, Charles decided, He would be hard pressed to deny so sweet a plea.

"Let her legs be okay, so she can run again," Lucy offered.

"And let her find all her friends and family," Jennifer added.

Alex and Robbie solemnly spread a blue towel over the top of the box where the rabbit lay. Then both of them looked up expectantly. There was a moment of silence before Josie piped up in a more cheerful tone.

"God bless us, everyone."

Lucy grimaced and gave her sister a patient look. "That's from a movie. Tiny Tim says it."

"So? I like it. God bless us, everyone," the child repeated.

As if her words let down a barrier, everyone seemed to relax.

"Yeah, God bless us, everyone," Alex echoed, grinning at Josie. "Did you ever think how cool it is that some dude wrote that hundreds of years ago and we still say it?"

"The power of words," Marilyn said as Joe picked up the small box and brought it into the kitchen. "That's what they mean by 'the pen is mightier than the sword.'"

"That's what I want to do," Alex admitted, sinking cross-legged onto the rug and picking up the guitar. "I want to write words—you know, to songs—that people will remember even after I'm not around."

Judith sat down across from her son with a curious look on her face. "I never knew that, Alex. Have you written anything like that yet?"

He ducked his head. "Not yet. I mean, I've written stuff. But nothing that's very good."

"My favorite words are from a poem," Marilyn said, joining the group near the hearth. "Do you know 'Maud Muller'? This part is near the end. 'For of all sad words of tongue or pen, the saddest are these: "It might have been."'" She shot Judith a wry look. "I told you I had a gypsy's soul. I guess I don't want to ever wonder what might have been. I want to have done it."

"Except for mountain climbing," Robbie quipped.

"Ha, ha," Marilyn retorted. "What about you, smart aleck? What words do you remember that you can never forget?"

"'Robbie, leave your sisters alone.'" He mimicked her voice, to the vast amusement of everyone but his mother. "'Robbie, do your chores,'" he added in a deeper tone as his dad came into the room.

"My favorite words from a book were in *Charlotte's*

Web," Jennifer said, ignoring Robbie's antics. "In the part when Charlotte first weaves the words over the pig. 'Some pig' she weaves to save Wilbur. It shows how good a friend she was. I always did like that. Only if I said 'some pig' to my best friend, she'd think I was insulting her."

"I remember that part!" Lucy cried. "It was so cool to think that animals and even insects could think and had feelings and everything."

"What words do you remember?" Jennifer prodded her friend. "Maybe it's something I read, too."

Lucy bit her lip as she thought. Then she laughed in embarrassment. "Do you play baseball? Or softball?" When Jennifer shook her head, Lucy sent her an apologetic look. "I know this doesn't seem like it means very much, but I like it. 'Mighty Casey has struck out.'"

Robbie hooted with laughter. "I could have guessed that! 'Mighty Casey has struck out.' You mean mighty Lucy has struck out!"

"It's not just about baseball, doofus! It's about real life," Lucy said, defending her choice. "Even if someone is a real hotshot and thinks he can't lose, he still can."

"That's a rather cynical outlook for a little girl."

Everyone looked over at Charles.

"What's cynical mean?" Lucy asked him, her gaze direct.

There was no reason for him to have said that, Charles berated himself. Now he had to get himself out of it gracefully. He shifted in his seat. "Cynical is the opposite of optimistic. People who are optimistic see the good in everyone and everything. They think everything is going to work out for the best. A cynical person always expects the worst. Or usually, he does. An optimist would expect Casey to hit a home run. A cynic expects him to strike out."

Lucy digested that a moment. "Okay, I think I get it. Which one are you?"

That stopped Charles cold. He glanced uneasily at Judith. "I . . . I would have to say that I'm an optimist. But not a cockeyed optimist," he hastened to add. "I wouldn't have succeeded in real estate development these past years if I wasn't both an optimist and a realist."

Once more he sought out Judith. She was watching him with an expressionless look on her face. Did she think the optimistic side of him was overriding the realist in expecting their marriage to recover? Was that what she was thinking?

Lucy nodded. "I think that's what I am, too," she decided. "I always hope for the best, but sometimes I know it's not going to turn out that way."

"What written words have you always remembered?" Joe directed the question to Charles.

Charles's jaw tightened. What was this, grill Charles Montgomery night?

"Nothing comes to mind at the moment. How about you, Judith?" He turned toward her, knowing the sarcastic edge in his voice was misdirected. "What words do you remember?"

Judith averted her head, staring down at her hands as she twisted one of her rings back and forth. For a moment Charles feared she would quote some frighteningly revealing words, something with a message for him. A message saying good-bye. His pulse quickened in the few seconds of silence. Then she raised her face and smiled ruefully.

"I doubt if any of you have ever heard these words. They're from a story that was written in *The Whole Earth Catalog,* back in the late sixties or early seventies."

"We have a copy of it still." Marilyn smiled encouragingly at Judith. "I vaguely remember an ongoing story running through the catalog."

" 'Divine Right's Trip,' " Judith threw in. "There's a line in it that has always stayed with me. A bit of graffiti D.R. reads somewhere. 'There are times when the wolves are silent and the moon is howling.' " She paused and shrugged. "Not a particularly well-known line, as I said."

"That's cool," Alex said thoughtfully. He nodded slowly. "Actually, that could be part of a really cool song. You know, the starting point for the lyrics."

Judith laughed. "Go for it, then."

"It's sort of like 'still waters run deep,' " Joe remarked. "I guess I'll have to dig out *The Whole Earth Catalog* and read D.R.'s story."

Maybe I should, too, Charles worried as he stared at his wife. He vaguely remembered that catalog from their college days, but Judith obviously remembered verbatim quotes from it. The fact that they could be so out of step was terrifying. And then there was the quote itself. Why had it stayed with her? What did it signify?

"Okay, it's your turn, Alex," Jennifer grinned at her brother. "Have you got any words? Probably lyrics, knowing him," she said to the rest of them.

"Yeah, probably," Alex agreed. "Trouble is, there's so much to choose from." He frowned as he searched his memory.

"Not 'Love in an elevator'?" Robbie asked in mock seriousness.

Alex laughed. "Dude, you read my mind," he quipped as the girls all giggled and the two mothers struggled to look reproving. "Aerosmith has a way with words. But no, seriously. There's this song. It goes, 'Imperfection makes for a perfect world.'" Alex hesitated. His face colored and he ducked his head. "I know it sounds weird, but it's true if you think about it. Everyone has their own ideas about the way things should be. You know, how to make everything just perfect. And we all think everybody else's ideas are wrong. That they're imperfect. But it's all those so-called imperfections that make this world so interesting. You know, different strokes for different folks." He shrugged and gave a self-conscious smile. "It's a pretty good song, too. The guitar work is way cool."

"And it was written by a heavy-metal group?" Joe asked Alex. His gaze, however, rested on Charles.

"Yeah. It's a new group called Divider," Alex replied. His eyes followed the direction of Joe's, and Charles automatically turned to meet his son's gaze. If Joe's watchfulness had aggravated him, however, Alex's wariness unnerved him. Part cautious, part belligerent, Alex's expression seemed to challenge his father, and Charles felt a deep pang of regret. He'd never meant for Alex to feel defensive around him. When they'd disagreed in the past, he'd never wanted Alex to feel that the disapproval was directed at him personally. It was the trappings Charles had disliked. The hair. The music. The pierced ear.

Yet Alex's caution made it clear he'd taken the criticisms to heart. How could Charles make him understand that he loved him? That none of the rest really mattered at all?

He swallowed hard and determinedly ignored the sudden pounding of his heart. "Are the words to most of those songs—you know, heavy-metal songs—that thought provoking?"

Alex held his father's gaze, seeming to search his face as he considered his answer. "Not usually," he finally conceded. "I mean, they almost always have a lot of emotion. You know, anger or frustration. Love. But the words are usually secondary to the music itself."

Charles nodded. "It's always pretty loud."

Alex chuckled. "It has to be. That's part of the emotions."

"Getting a headache from the noise is a part of it, you see," Robbie threw in. "If your head hurts, then you'll be angrier and more frustrated."

"Dork." Alex grinned and shoved Robbie. "We all know what kind of music you like. 'Grandma got run over by a reindeer.' " He mimicked Robbie's higher-pitched singing voice.

"Yeah, and you're just a sentimental kind of guy. Playing 'Silent Night' and all."

Charles broke into Robbie's teasing. "He did a great job of it."

Alex studied his father as if he could not quite understand his sudden defense—and approval. "It's an emotional song. That's what I like in music. Expressing emotions in words and on the guitar."

" 'Imperfection makes for a perfect world.' " Judith repeated the lyrics Alex had offered. "That's worth remembering for those times when we can see things only our own way, and dismiss everybody else as being foolish."

"Come on, Mom. When have you ever called anyone a fool?" Jennifer scoffed. "You're the one who always makes peace between everyone."

Judith's eyes flitted to Charles, then settled back on their daughter. "Well, let's say I try. But, hey, how did we get off the subject? Come on, Robbie, Joe. Neither of you have told us your favorite line from the written word. Who's first?"

Charles didn't listen to Robbie's answer. He didn't laugh when everyone else did. And he only vaguely heard Joe's comments about a book called *Ecotopia* and its impact on him. He was too wrapped up in his own dark thoughts.

Up to now Judith *had* always been the peacemaker, the one to see merit in both sides of every situation. She'd been the one who saw beyond people's imperfections, while he'd been the one who always demanded perfection. But it was only *his* vision of what would be perfect, with no allowances for anyone else's. It was devastating to admit that he didn't know how his own family saw the world, or what they wanted from it. He didn't know the people he lived with and loved and spoke to every day of his life.

He'd seen a heavy-metal head, as Jennifer was so fond of calling Alex. But what he'd missed was the poet.

He'd seen a picture-perfect wife who made him look good. But he'd missed the woman who wanted something more from her life than that.

He knew what Alex wanted. At least he thought he did. If he just let up a little and accepted that the boy was serious about his music, he was certain things would improve between them. As for Jennifer, well, he would have to prove to her that he could handle the important matters, too. He would spend more time with her, and eventually it would happen.

But he didn't have any idea what Judith wanted.

He peered sidelong at his wife, studying her as she took Josie onto her lap and let the child teach her a clapping game. He had not attempted to talk to her about their differences since the Walkers had arrived. Perhaps it had been cowardice on his part. But he couldn't put it off any longer. Tonight, once they went up to bed, they would talk. He would wait for her, no matter how she sought to avoid him. He would suggest that the kids sleep downstairs tonight. Then he and Judith would pin down the problem and begin to work out a solution. He was not going to lose her. Not now, when he realized how desperately he loved and needed her.

Chapter

Twelve

Judith frowned, trying to remember which gift was in which box. The green paisley box was an "America Rocks" T-shirt for Alex, but would it be too big for Robbie? And which package held the videocassettes of *The Wizard of Oz* and *Pretty Woman*? She'd put them in a much bigger box to fool Jennifer. Then she hesitated. If she gave them to Lucy, would the Walkers have a VCR to play them on?

She sighed and slumped down on the bed, a crease forming across her brow.

"What's wrong?"

She jumped in surprise when Charles's voice broke

into her thoughts. "Oh. Well, I was . . . I was trying to pick which gifts to give the Walker children. Marilyn and I discussed some of the items, but I forgot to ask her whether they had a VCR or not."

Charles moved across the chilly room toward the fireplace, and held his hands out to the flames. "I heard Josie say something about being too old to watch her *Sesame Street* tapes anymore, so they must. You know, I don't think they're quite so out of touch with modern life as I first thought." He turned to look at her, a rueful expression on his face. "To tell the truth, they're a pretty nice family."

Judith quirked a brow at him. "Yes, they are."

"But you're surprised I admit it," Charles finished her thought for her.

"Well . . ." Judith sighed, then nodded. "I suppose that's true. You didn't seem too pleased to have them here. And it's obvious Joe sometimes rubs you the wrong way."

"Yeah. Well, he's awfully patronizing at times. He's way too smug, considering—" He broke off. But Judith knew what he'd been about to say.

"Considering that he's an itinerant artist who can't make much more than a ditchdigger would—minimum wage. Right?"

"I didn't say that."

"Yes, but you thought it."

To her surprise, he did not argue the point. "Sometimes I judge people by standards that are too . . . well, the wrong standards for them."

Judith stared at him, more surprised than ever. "Yes," she slowly agreed. "Sometimes you do."

"Anyway, I'm actually kind of glad they ended up

on our doorstep." He stopped then and only looked at her as if he were waiting for her reaction to that.

He was going to give it his all, she realized at once. He was going to be humble, apologetic, and sincere tonight. In short, he was planning to give her the hard sell. Charles was a masterful salesman. That's what made him such a good real estate developer. He let Doug handle most of the construction side of the work, while he handled the personalities involved— the politicians, bankers, and unions. He could sell flour to a wheat farmer, and now he was planning to sell her on the idea that he could change.

She lifted her chin a notch, and a bitter smile thinned her lips. "I'm glad they came, too. They've been good for Jennifer and Alex."

"They've been good for me, too, Jude. I mean, everything is so Christmasy now. The tree, the caroling. If they hadn't been here, I'm not so sure we could have created the same feelings. I *know* we couldn't have."

He shifted slightly, and Judith realized that he was actually uneasy. She stared at him harder. Charles was never uneasy when he was selling an idea. She'd heard him say a thousand times that you had to be truly excited about something to be able to effectively sell someone else on it. Your enthusiasm had to be real. It couldn't be faked, or else it would show.

But he was uneasy now, and she wasn't sure exactly what that meant. She reached for a large box wrapped in red paper with a huge green bow and shook it. If he wanted to cut to the heart of the matter, so be it. "You're probably right," she replied slowly. "You and I would have had a difficult time creating the illusion of happiness and family warmth that comes so naturally to the Walkers."

She met his eyes and saw the pain in them. It took all her willpower not to crumple in the face of it, for she didn't want to hurt him. She was just tired of always being second to M.G., Inc. She wanted to be first with someone. If it couldn't be with him, then it would have to be with herself. She was going to put herself first. She wanted to be happy. If that meant they had to be apart, then she was ready to make that move.

There was an awkward silence. Charles shifted his weight once more. "We used to be able to do that, to create that happiness in our own family. I . . . I think it's something we could learn to do again. If we both try," he added.

Judith steeled herself against the rush of feelings his emotion-filled words generated. She forced herself to be cool and analytical. "I think, Charles, that our concepts of trying are vastly different. You do all the things you think a good husband and father should do. We live well. But . . ." Her composure slipped despite her best efforts to remain calm. "But I find myself more and more dissatisfied with it."

"But why?" he interrupted, beginning to grow angry. "What do you want from me—" He broke off suddenly, and drew back—recoiled, it seemed, as his face went pale. "Is it . . . is it someone else?"

Judith could not hide her shock. "No! No, how can you even think such a ridiculous thing?" She stood up and began to pace as her own anger surfaced. "How very like you to assume such a thing! You can't conceive of any flaw in your own behavior, so you look for something despicable like that in mine!"

"Judith, I didn't mean—"

"Oh, yes, you did. In fact, you'd probably like it a lot better if I *had* carried on with some other man. Then you would be absolved of any fault. You could be the innocent one. The injured one!"

She drew a shuddering breath, all thoughts of maintaining control gone, and turned an accusing face on him. "The disloyalty is yours, Charles. The infidelity."

"I swear, I never, Judith. Not once in all these years—"

She laughed, only it was the saddest and most miserable sound she'd ever made. "Every day, Charles. You and your business. You and your office phone with an extension in our bedroom. The bigger you got, the bigger you needed to be. The more successful your hard work was, the harder you worked. If M.G., Inc., was a woman, I'd have a hell of a lot better chance of getting you back. But M.G., Inc., is a disease. And you're terminal. *We're* terminal."

The silence was awful. Judith's pulse beat hard and fast in her ears. Roared, it seemed. She thought insanely of the rabbit, Roger Rabbit, lying in that box, gasping out her last breath. Dying silently, though everyone there wanted her to live.

That's what she was witnessing now. No matter how much they all wanted it to live, their marriage was dying. It was gasping out its last breath in a cold bedroom in the middle of a blizzard. By morning it would be dead.

She swallowed the hard lump in her throat and stared at Charles. His face was white, his disbelief plain.

He shook his head. "You're wrong. You're wrong.

You mean more to me than the company. How can you think you don't? I mean, I won't deny I spend a lot of time working. I . . . I guess I'm a workaholic. But if I'd known you felt this way—"

"What would you have done? Scaled back? Maybe abandoned the new hotel project?" She gave him a bitter smile. "That hotel is what you've been aiming at for years. The pinnacle. But when it's done, what will you do next? Something bigger and better, no doubt. Something that will prove you even more successful, and make you even richer. Do you know, Charles, that you could quit your job today and we'd still never want for anything, not if we scaled back our lifestyle to a reasonable level. We'd never want for anything. Not food. Not shelter. Not anything.

"Of course, you'd be miserable if you quit working. And I'm miserable if you continue." She shrugged, trying desperately to regain some level of composure. "So where does that leave us?"

His brows had begun to lower as she talked. Outrage had obviously taken the place of his initial shock. Outrage and denial. "We're not terminal, dammit! The whole point of this trip is to mend the rifts in our marriage, but you have been determined from the outset not even to give us a chance. My God, Judith, haven't the past two days proven my point? We *can* be happy together—"

"With someone forcing us to be," she interrupted. "With the phones out and no way for you to work."

She knew she'd scored with that, for he ran his hand distractedly through his hair as he groped for a response.

"Okay. Okay. I work too much. I can change that. I

can," he repeated in the face of her skeptical expression.

"It's more than that, Charles. I used that as . . . I don't know. As an example. It's a symptom, though. Not the whole problem. You need a constant challenge to be happy. You need to struggle and win to feel complete. And I . . ." She swallowed and shook her head.

"You married me knowing I was that way. That's what attracted you in the beginning."

"Yes, I know it did. And I know you think I'm being terribly unfair now."

"Selfish," he accused. "Selfish is the word. What about Alex and Jennifer? What are you going to tell them? Mommy doesn't like living in a big house and having so many privileges and luxuries. So she's decided to divorce Daddy. Is that what you're going to tell them?"

Judith stiffened. "I'm going to tell them that I can't fit into the role you want me to play. I know Alex, of all people, will understand *that*."

To her surprise, that seemed to affect him more than anything else she'd said. Before her eyes he seemed to shrink as the anger fled him. She watched as he crossed to the bed and slowly lowered himself to sit on it. When he stared up at her, his face was stripped of all pretense and protective emotions. She saw pain and fear in his eyes, and it sent a shiver of fear through her as well. For a brief, insightful moment she recognized how much she'd always relied on his strength. His confidence and enthusiasm had always carried her along, and she'd been willing to take that ride. But now he was the vulnerable one, and she was strong.

Was it fair of her to abandon him now just because she finally had the ability to do so?

Judith sat down too as thoughts of past discussions at her roundtable flashed through her mind. Dominant partners; shifts of power; balance in a relationship. She'd participated in those talks, thinking at the time that she understood. But she hadn't. She'd thought Charles the dominant partner in their relationship, the one who made the big decisions. The one whose needs and goals set the pattern for their marriage. She hadn't even recognized her own dissatisfaction until the past few years. But now as he sat here before her at his most vulnerable, she realized that she did wield a certain power.

He'd never wielded his power with the intention of hurting her. How could she wield hers any less generously?

She reached over and placed her hand over his. "I know all this seems terrible. It's not part of the future you've always envisioned for us. But you will survive this, Charles. You'll see. We'll both be better people for it. Better parents, too."

His hand turned over beneath hers and his fingers slipped between hers. Palm to palm, they held hands.

"I'll never survive," he whispered. Tears glistened in his dark eyes. "I'll never survive. I wouldn't want to."

He gathered her into an awkward embrace, and for a long trembling moment they clung together.

There was comfort in his arms, Judith recognized as she leaned against him. The comfort of familiarity. The comfort of knowing you were loved. And there was that same familiar response deep inside her, the part that had always loved his touch. His kiss.

He was kissing her now—her hair, her ear, her cheek—and a small voice in her head told her to pull away. But she couldn't. Charles needed her. The truth was, she needed him, too. At least, right now she did. As for tomorrow . . .

She turned her face up to his, aware that her cheeks were wet with both his tears and her own.

"Judith, Judith. You can't leave me . . ." His embrace became desperate, and as they met in a shattering kiss, she feared he was right.

They lay together a long while later, side by side in the big bed, warm from each other and the heavy feather comforter. Charles's arm was under her neck, and her right cheek lay very near his heart. It was a position they'd lain in more times than she could ever count. The silence was mutual, and in the drowsy aftermath of their loving, Judith could almost believe everything was fine.

Charles, however, had not lost sight of reality. He did not assume their lovemaking had solved their differences, as was normally his approach. She heard him sigh, and his arm tightened slightly around her shoulder.

"Jude, tell me. If you could have one thing for Christmas—one wish or whatever, what would it be?"

Judith stared into the dim shadows of the room, the gray corners where the fading firelight did not reach. "I . . . well. That's difficult to say." She smiled sadly against his shoulder. "There's not a lot I don't have."

"I'm not talking about jewelry or cars. You know that. I'm talking about the things you want. The things that I don't know about."

Judith lay there without speaking, searching her mind for something. What she wanted was a direction of her own. But that was not what he wanted to hear. When the words came, she was as startled by them as he was.

"I want our old house. The first one. Remember? Where we turned the garage into an office."

"On Cleveland Avenue? But it was tiny. And I think it's been turned into a beauty parlor. That neighborhood has been going downhill for a long time."

Judith shook her head. She didn't want to own it again. She knew that would be pointless. But she wanted to feel like she had when they had lived there so long ago. "We were happy there."

"We outgrew it long before we moved out. And you . . . you hated that kitchen. It was a corridor, with no storage space and ugly turquoise countertops."

"It was an ugly little house," Judith conceded. "But it has come to symbolize—" She broke off as emotions flooded her heart. "We were happy there," she repeated softly.

Charles turned to her, clutching her painfully close. "I'd move back there if I thought it would really make you happy," he choked out.

They fell asleep in each other's arms. Or at least Charles did. Judith lay awake for a long time, listening to the faint crackling from the fire and the silence of the house. Even the wind had stopped. The house might have been floating somewhere in space, cushioned in the clouds.

It *was* Christmas Eve, she thought fancifully. It was a time of rebirth and salvation. Of angels bending near the earth.

Then her eyes flew open. There were still gifts to place under the tree.

As carefully as she could, she crept out of the bed. The cold in the room was like a slap in the face, and she scrambled into her robe and slippers. Then she gathered up the gifts she'd sorted and made her way downstairs.

She ducked under the curtain at the base of the stairwell, concentrating on the packages stacked so precariously in her arms. When she saw Marilyn sitting near the hearth, she straightened up in surprise. They shared a smile. Then Judith made her way to the Christmas tree and laid the gaily wrapped presents around its base.

"What are you doing still up?" she whispered, crossing to sit on the hearth next to Marilyn.

The woman smiled. "I guess you could say I'm counting my blessings."

Judith looked over the sleeping group. Jennifer and Lucy were curled up on a couch. Joe was sprawled under several blankets on the sofa. Josie's curly head was visible there, too. The two boys were bedded down in the corner.

"They certainly are blessings," she agreed with a smile of her own.

"You're pretty blessed yourself," Marilyn said softly.

Judith sighed. "I am." She stared at her hands, twisting her wedding band around and around. "I have so much. More than most women ever even hope to get. I suppose I should be more content."

"Do you really believe we're meant to be perfectly content?" Marilyn murmured. "If you stop and think about all the people we most admire, I doubt you'd find a contented one in the lot. That's what makes them so admirable. They struggled for change, or for knowledge, or acceptance. I mean, if any of the people in the history books had been content with their lot, where would mankind be?"

"But I don't want to be a leader."

"You want to change the status quo—*your* status quo."

Judith considered her words. "I want to change my status quo, yes. But only a little. Just so that I can finally be content."

Marilyn gave her an understanding smile. "Well, that's commendable. But I'm not so sure you have to throw the baby out with the bathwater."

A part of Judith resented the personal nature of Marilyn's comment. But then Jennifer turned over in her sleep, and as Judith stared at her daughter, she wondered if maybe Marilyn was right. "I suppose that's how it appears."

"Tell me what would make you happy. With Charles," Marilyn added.

Judith shrugged. "That's what's so hard about this. I don't know."

"Okay, let's start with the basics. Do you like where you live?"

"We have a beautiful house."

"But do you like living in it?"

With a faint groan, Judith swept the hair back from her face. "It's . . . well, it's a boring place. Big pretentious houses on big manicured lots in an exclusive neighborhood."

"White bread." Marilyn chuckled. "You've obviously had too much white bread. What you need is some dark pumpernickel. Some German rye. Or maybe cracked wheat or oatmeal raisin."

Judith laughed. "Oatmeal raisin? What in heaven's name are you talking about?"

"Have you considered moving into the center of town? Living in an old town house with a neighborhood grocery and restaurants? With old people and young people, and rich and poor all living side by side?" Her brows raised questioningly. "That would certainly not be white bread."

It was a novel idea, and Judith found it perversely appealing. But as in everything else, there was more to consider than just her own wishes. "Charles would never go for it. And the children. They're in such terrific schools where we live now. I couldn't take them out and put them with—"

She broke off, embarrassed by what she'd almost said. But Marilyn knew.

"Put them in a school with just anybody? Put them in with children less privileged than they are? With kids whose parents might be domestic workers, shopkeepers? Itinerant artists?" She smiled. "I don't think you're giving Alex and Jennifer enough credit, Judith. And maybe not Charles either. I'm not saying that living in an old urban environment is the best solution for you. It's just an out-of-the-blue idea. But I do think you're ignoring a lot of solutions just because they're unconventional. And yet it sounds to me like it's convention you're really rebelling against."

Judith stared at Marilyn for a long moment. There was enormous sense in what she said. Enormous insight. She pursed her lips thoughtfully. "Have you ever fallen into that rut—you know, of being conventional?"

After a long pause of her own, Marilyn smiled. "I fear I was *too* unconventional. I took delight in breaking all the rules. Doing nothing that was expected of me."

"You? I know you said you were a gypsy at heart. But you seem so, well, so reliable. So strong and . . . and motherly."

"It's funny you should say that. Before you came downstairs, I was thinking that Christmas Eve we should be celebrating motherhood. Giving birth and all the pain and joy that goes along with it. You know, I hope I am a good mother. I try to be, and my children have turned out in a way that makes me proud. But mothering takes flexibility more than strength. You've got to go with the flow, and the more kids you have, the more directions the flow goes. Being a gypsy is not inconsistent with being a good parent. Kids are such adaptable little creatures."

"What about husbands?"

"Husbands." Marilyn chuckled. "Now there's a funny creature. Wonderful. Exasperating. Tell me, does Charles love you?"

Judith was momentarily taken aback by the directness of Marilyn's question. But she knew the answer. Charles had shown her the raw truth of his feelings upstairs.

"Yes, he loves me," she admitted, not sure whether that should make her smile or cry.

"Do you love him?"

Judith didn't have to ponder the answer to that question. It came automatically to her lips, but she knew it was more than merely a habitual response.

"Yes. I do. But . . . well, that's what makes things so confusing. I love him, but sometimes I just want to burst free of him. Of my family, too," she added in a barely discernible whisper.

Marilyn did not respond to that, but Judith didn't find the silence oppressive. Marilyn was not the judgmental sort. It struck her with sudden clarity that she would love to have her as a neighbor—as a friend. It would be good to have her children as friends for Alex and Jennifer, too. They already had too many white bread friends. Maybe Marilyn had something there.

Judith took a long slow breath, aware of the scent of the fire and the Christmas tree. She looked over at it, towering in its corner, marked only faintly by the glint of the firelight on the many glass ornaments. Every Christmas tree she'd ever seen had been beautiful in its own right. But this one was even more so. Maybe it was the joy that had gone into decorating it. The children had been so happy and unrestrained, in a way they seldom were.

It was that joy she wanted in her life once more, she realized. The joy of simply being alive and with the people she loved most. Was it possible for her to make it happen?

As if she sensed Judith's question, Marilyn spoke. "A woman's lot is a difficult one. Our mothers had it hard in one respect; they had very few choices open to them. They married and stayed home to raise kids. Our generation has been given the choice to do otherwise. But often we're pressured into choices we don't want, by the very movement that speaks for us. If we don't live up to our potential as people with careers, we're branded as failures as women."

"In my social circle, the women don't work for the money. They do it for the prestige or the power. Or they control charitable institutions that generally manage to provide the social contacts important to their husbands' careers."

"Don't get me wrong, Judith. I'm not saying being a career woman is right or wrong. Nor am I saying the Junior League crowd is wrong. Whatever gives you a feeling of accomplishment and being needed is what's right for you. We all have to make some compromises. None of us get everything we want. But we don't get *anything* if we don't work hard in some way for it."

Judith nodded. "The difficult part is knowing what you want."

"I think you know already what you want. You're just not sure how to get it."

Judith thought once more how much she'd love to have Marilyn as a neighbor, then turned abruptly to face her. "If I do it—if I convince Charles to move to a real neighborhood, will you come to visit us?"

Marilyn smiled, and even in the shadows of the room, Judith felt the warm and peaceful reassurance that exuded from her.

"If you mean, will we stay friends after this Christmas is over, of course we will." She reached over and took Judith's hand. "We'll always be friends."

Chapter Thirteen

Charles was awakened by the incessant flashing of the digital clock radio on the night table just beyond his nose. Like a beacon light, it imprinted itself on his eyelids until he reluctantly opened them. The electricity must have gone off briefly during the night, he thought blearily. They would have to reset all the clocks now. Then he remembered where he was and came fully awake. The electricity had come back on. They would have heat again! The storm was over.

Even as he lay there, he heard the soft whooshing noise of the central heating unit kicking back on. By morning the house would be warm again.

He blinked and looked around. It was still dark, and still almost as cold inside as it was outside. Christmas was here, he realized. In the morning they would all get up and open gifts. Then they would fix a great Christmas dinner. It would be perfect. At least he would try his damnedest to make it perfect, he amended.

He turned slightly to look at Judith, and the events of the evening came rushing back to him. They had made love with more emotion than he could ever recall. He'd thought she was going to leave him, but then she'd come to him with such urgency he'd begun to hope again. She *did* love him, he told himself. She still loved him, and as long as she did, there was a chance for them. She might not believe it yet, but he would prove it to her. When she saw what was in the Tiffany box—

Charles halted in the process of turning to curl around Judith. When she saw what was in the Tiffany box, she would be disappointed. He knew it with depressing certainty. Sapphires in a platinum setting were not what she wanted from him. He was beginning to understand that now. But what could he do about it at this late hour?

With a silent curse at his own stupidity, he swung his legs over the side of the bed, ignoring the frigid temperature of the room. He would have to retrieve the gift from its spot beneath the tree. If Judith saw it, it would only serve as proof in her eyes that he just didn't understand. He found his robe and slippers, and then, with a last glance at his wife, eased out of the room.

In the living room the children were still asleep. But Joe and Marilyn were not on the sofa-sleeper.

Charles followed a narrow beam of light to the kitchen.

"What are you two doing up?" he asked as he closed the door behind him.

"Good morning." Marilyn smiled a greeting at him. She reached for a mug and immediately poured him a cup from the coffeemaker.

"What time is it?" Charles inquired, taking the warm mug gratefully between his cold hands.

"About five-thirty," Joe answered. "The electricity came on around five, and I've been hearing what sounds like snowplows down the mountain. They should be clearing the highway pretty soon."

Charles took a slow sip of the steaming coffee. "I'm glad I don't have their job. Especially on Christmas morning."

"Yeah. But they know how important their work is. There will be a lot of people grateful to them this Christmas."

Charles stared at Joe, trying to determine whether he was trying to make some point with his words. But to his surprise, Charles discovered that he didn't really care. He was willing to concede that some blue-collar guy, who drove a snowplow for barely a living wage, was just as important in the scheme of things as anyone else. "Yeah, a lot of people will be grateful," he agreed with a thoughtful nod.

Marilyn moved toward Joe and he put his arm around her shoulder. "What are you doing up so early?" he asked Charles.

For a moment Charles wasn't sure how to answer. But Marilyn smiled at him so encouragingly, and even Joe's interest no longer seemed antagonizing or condescending. With a sigh Charles perched on one of the chrome stools.

"I woke up. I guess it was the digital clock. Then I got to thinking, and . . ." He trailed off, uneasy about admitting the truth to them. But for once he pushed himself to go on. "I, uh . . . I decided that the gift I bought Judith is, well . . . that it's not appropriate. I mean, well, I don't think she'll like it."

In the brief uncomfortable silence, Charles had the oddest feeling that for once they both approved of him. Even more odd, he wasn't infuriated by the thought of them passing such judgment one way or the other on him.

"Do you have something else in mind?" Marilyn asked.

"Not really," Charles confessed. "What can I get her now? I guess I'll just give her an IOU. You know, promise her a trip somewhere. Together, just us two," he added. "Yeah, that's a good idea. She'd like something like that."

Joe nodded. "Yes, she probably would."

Marilyn took a long sip of coffee. "My favorite gift that Joe ever gave me was a painting he did of the first house we lived in way back in college."

"It wasn't much of a painting," Joe demurred. "And not too accurate either. I did it from memory."

Marilyn smiled. "Yes. We had rented the place although it was barely more than a shack. But it was slated for demolition—to build an apartment complex, as I recall. Anyway, we had to move, and I cried for days. So Joe did a painting for me." She looked up at her husband with such undisguised love that Charles was almost embarrassed to witness it. But it was the sort of look he wanted to receive from Judith, so he pressed on.

"It's hard to know what someone else wants. Really wants," he emphasized.

"I guess you have to really listen," Marilyn said. "I mean, I knew I couldn't have our little house back. And Joe knew he couldn't get it back for me. So he gave me the painting as a good memory of it. And in the process, he showed me he understood how I felt. That's what meant the most to me."

Charles swallowed, remembering what Judith had said last night about the old house on Cleveland Avenue. "Why did that place—you said it was a shack. Why did it mean so much to you?"

Marilyn shrugged. "I came from a family that, well, let's just say we weren't the ideal family unit. That little house was the first place where I really felt surrounded by love—and able to love freely as well. That's so important. I guess I let that house symbolize happiness to me, and when it was demolished, I felt like my happiness was being demolished, too. Of course, I soon learned that wasn't the case." She leaned her head against Joe. "Love and happiness don't require a place. They require people."

Then she grinned sheepishly. "How did we get on this subject, anyway? Come on, Joe. We need to get breakfast going and wake up the children."

Charles's head was spinning with too many confusing thoughts to understand what they were up to. All he could think was that he had to show Judith that he understood—that he wanted more than anything in the world to shower her with love and happiness. What could he give her that could make that clear?

He stared blankly at the kitchen window, hardly

seeing the earliest hint of dawn that let the silhouette of the forest vaguely separate from the dark sky. He didn't know how to paint. Maybe he could hire someone. No, that wouldn't work. He was beginning to understand that this had to come from him, and him alone.

Not until Marilyn began to make a pot of oatmeal did he pull his thoughts away from his own predicament. "Why are you making breakfast so early? No one's up yet. They probably won't be for hours."

"We have to get going," she said as she placed bowls on the counter and opened a drawer to find spoons. "The snowplows are coming, and if we can get back to our van, they'll help us back onto the road."

"What?" Charles stood up, appalled that they could be thinking of leaving. "You can't go now. It's still dark. And it's Christmas morning—" He shook his head, searching for some argument that could dissuade her.

Just then Joe returned to the kitchen with Josie in his arms and Lucy and Robbie in tow. "I'll get these guys dressed, Marilyn. How long till breakfast? I don't want to miss those snowplows."

"I'll be ready in less than five minutes."

"Okay, gang. You heard your mom. Let's hustle and get dressed. And be quiet about it. We don't want to wake everybody."

Charles watched in dismay as the Walker family made their hasty preparations. As stunned as he was by their impending departure in the predawn hours, however, he was even more amazed at his own regret. He didn't want them to leave as much for his own sake as for theirs.

"It's freezing out there," he argued as the children

sat down to their oatmeal. "And the snow is too deep —and too dangerous."

But his words fell on deaf ears. The kitchen was a flurry of activity as the Walkers donned their boots and coats, mufflers, hats, and gloves. Only when he realized they were going no matter what he said, did he accept defeat.

"At least let me wake up Judith and the kids. They'll want to tell you good-bye."

Marilyn stood up after fastening Josie's coat. "You tell them good-bye for us, Charles. And tell them thank you for everything."

He stared at her as a panicky feeling swept over him. "We're the ones who should be thanking you," he whispered, knowing without a doubt that it was true. "You've made our stay here . . ." He ran a hand through his hair. During the past two days the Walkers had helped his own family to function as a family again. But now that they were leaving, he was terrified everything would fall apart again. He would never be able to keep Judith if they left now.

But Marilyn seemed almost to know his fears, for she laid a reassuring hand on his arm. "Your heart is in the right place, Charles. You let logic get in the way sometimes, but we all do that every now and again. Just relax a little more and everything will be all right."

He could not pretend he didn't understand. His pride mattered nothing at all when his family was on the line. "I wish I could be so sure," he whispered, fighting down his panic.

"A good marriage takes a lot of listening and hard work. I know you're willing to work at it. The hardest thing for most of us is the listening."

Those last words stayed with Charles as they all slipped out the kitchen door. Joe broke a trail through the virgin snow, holding Josie in his arms. Robbie and Lucy followed, while Marilyn brought up the rear. Charles stood on the back deck watching them trudge out of sight, shivering in the icy stillness.

The wind was not blowing. The sky was clear, with the last of the stars fading as it slowly lightened. The snow-covered ground was a vague violet, edged by the black silhouettes of the trees. As the Walkers made their laborious way down the long drive, they slowly faded into the shadowy dawn. Once he thought Marilyn might have turned and waved. But he blinked, and then he couldn't see them at all. They were gone.

A violent shiver shook him, and with a resigned sigh Charles turned back to the house. He hoped they were warm enough, and that the snowplows he could hear in the distance came upon their van soon. What if it wouldn't start? Maybe they'd come back then.

But Charles had a sinking feeling that the Walkers were gone for good. And he was unprepared for the profound sorrow that knowledge caused him.

Still, there was nothing he could do about that, he decided as he opened the kitchen door. They had their own lives to live, and his family had theirs. He had to go on from where he was. That was the stoic philosophy he used in business, and that's what he needed to cling to now.

He went over to the coffeemaker and poured another mugful. The Walkers had shown them how good family unity could feel. All he had to do was not let his family forget that lesson. They had to do things together more—spend more time together doing small stuff. Puzzles. Charades. Talking.

But that still did not solve the immediate problem of Judith's Christmas gift.

He put the mug down and swiftly fetched the exquisitely wrapped package from beneath the tree. As he did so, he spotted the electrical plug for the Christmas tree lights. On impulse he plugged it in, then sat back on his heels as the tiny twinkling lights came on.

It was a beautiful tree, he decided as a wave of sentiment washed over him. Jennifer shifted on the couch and rolled over, pulling the quilt over her head. Alex slept like a rock in the corner where he and Robbie had bedded down side by side last night.

Alex would probably enjoy going camping, Charles thought. They all would. As soon as it warmed up a bit, he would plan a camping trip for them all.

But would Judith agree to go? She wasn't much of an outdoor person anymore. When they'd first been married she'd enjoyed hiking. He frowned at the memory. She'd enjoyed gardening, too. But he'd hired a gardener years ago. And they never stayed any place where hiking was an option. Their trips always were associated with business, and were always in dense urban areas.

He clutched the Tiffany box tighter. Okay, a trip to a rural area. Maybe Florida. Or the Caribbean. They would frolic in the great outdoors like children, and she would see how much he loved her. And discover how much she still could love him.

With a sigh of relief Charles stood up. It was reassuring to have some sense of direction. Some plan of action. He shook the box as an idea came to him, and an optimistic grin lifted his face. Judith Montgomery was in for the toughest battle of her life, he vowed. She was not going to get away from him. She almost had, but like John Paul Jones, he had just begun to fight.

Vivid sunshine woke Judith, bright and almost blinding against her eyelids. She rolled over, shoving the comforter down from her shoulders. It was enough to smother a person, she thought groggily.

Very slowly did reality intrude. It was morning. Christmas morning. The sun was out; that meant the storm was over. And she was too warm. Who had tampered with the thermostat?

She woke up fully at the realization that the heat was indeed on. They had power again. With a huge yawn and an arching stretch she smiled. Thank heaven. While they'd not really suffered without electricity, having it back would certainly make cooking that turkey easier.

She looked around at the spacious bedroom. The morning sun slanted through the high clerestory window. It glinted off the snow outside as well, creating an almost unearthly brightness in the pale-colored room. How an interiors photographer would love this light, she thought fancifully. The elegant room. The rumpled bed that hinted so boldly at what had gone on the night before.

As she remembered last night, her contented smile faded, to be replaced by uncertainty. Last night she and Charles had made love in a way she couldn't begin to understand. It had been desperate at first, and then almost violent. But it had left her completely satisfied, both physically and emotionally. She'd been exhausted and beyond rational thought when they'd finally collapsed in a tangle of sheets and comforters and each other.

During that time they'd been beyond the conflicts of daily life and the accumulated baggage of twenty years together. For that brief time they'd simply been Judith and Charles, two people who loved each other in every way it is possible to love.

Just remembering the absolute perfection of it brought tears to her eyes.

Yet she was not fool enough to think that last night had actually changed anything—that everything that was wrong with their marriage had suddenly been made right. Charles might believe it was that easy, but she knew better.

Still, she could not honestly say that things were the same, either.

Feeling undeniably nervous, she rose and headed for the bathroom. A hot shower was true luxury, she decided as she hurried through her toilette. Clean hair, clothes that weren't piled on for warmth, and a sunny day. By the time she made her way down the stairs her good spirits had taken hold again. She was a little reluctant to face Charles, but she couldn't help thinking it was the most beautiful Christmas morning she'd ever seen.

The living room was deserted, but voices came from the kitchen and Judith headed that way. Charles, Alex, and Jennifer were in the midst of preparing a breakfast of toast, orange juice, and scrambled eggs, but the Walkers were nowhere to be seen.

"Good morning." She touched Jennifer's shoulder and reached up to tousle Alex's hair. Then she met Charles's gaze.

Only a second or two went by at most. Yet in that meeting of their eyes, a lifetime of emotion seemed to pass. It was awkward, but no more so than any first meeting between a man and woman, where the attraction exists yet is still too tentative to express. How odd to feel that way with her own husband. And yet something told her it was the right way to feel.

Her eyes lowered shyly, and it was then that Jennifer spoke up.

"They're gone, Mom. They left before we got up. All of them."

"What? Do you mean the Walkers?" Judith looked around in disbelief, sure that Jennifer was mistaken. "But that makes no sense. Why would they leave? *How* could they leave?"

"Joe heard the snowplows on the highway. He wanted to catch them so they could pull their van back onto the road." Charles shook his head. "I tried to talk them out of it, but they wouldn't listen. They left shortly before dawn."

Judith made her way to one of the stools and sat down. "But I don't understand."

"I don't either," he confessed, his brow creased in concern.

"We were going to have such a great Christmas," Jennifer complained. "Now everything is ruined."

"No, it's not," Alex countered. "I'm as mad as you are that they left, but I guess they figured they had a good reason. Maybe they had grandparents or somebody waiting for them. Anyway, it's still Christmas and we can still have a good day with just us."

Judith stared at her son, hearing the mixture of confidence and fear in his voice. He wanted the day to be good, and that alone bolstered her spirits. Two days ago he wouldn't have cared one way or the other. But he was scared, too, that they might not succeed.

She shifted her gaze to Jennifer, seeing the anxious expression on her young face, and it helped strengthen her conviction. Her children had learned a lot from the Walkers' brief presence in their lives. They knew now how satisfying family life could be. Was she going to let them be disappointed now? They were willing to try. So was Charles. It remained only for her to pitch in, too.

Her eyes met Charles's once more, and a slow smile lifted her lips. "Yes, though we all wish they could have stayed, we can still have a lovely Christmas just the same."

They ate breakfast in the living room with the tree twinkling behind them, beckoning them to partake of the bounty beneath it. The mound of gifts was truly impressive, but Charles good-naturedly dictated that they must finish their breakfast first. They would need that breakfast to furnish all the energy they would need for the huge task of opening all those presents.

As soon as the dishes were in the dishwasher, Jennifer planted herself at the base of the tree and began to pick up and shake the gifts. "This one's for you, Alex. And here's one for me." She giggled and glanced at her parents. "And this one . . ." Her happy expression faded. "This one's for Josie." She stared at her mother. "What should we do with it?"

"Just put it aside for now, honey. We'll decide later what to do with the Walkers' gifts."

"Maybe we could mail them the gifts," Alex suggested. "They live in a place called Edgard. I never heard of it, but it can't be too hard to find. We could mail them their gifts, and maybe they would write back to us."

"We could invite them to visit us," Jennifer threw in. "Hey, we could even meet them here again next year for Christmas!"

Judith met Charles's gaze and recognized the same mixture of love and hopefulness in it that she felt inside. Their children would never forget this Christmas. In spite of anything else the future might hold, there would always be fond memories of this Christmas and their unexpected guests.

"Those are both good ideas, kids. What do you say, Jude? Wouldn't you like to spend next Christmas here and invite the Walkers to join us?"

Judith hesitated. Though simply phrased, his question was loaded with subjects she was not quite ready to address. He wanted to know if they would be together next Christmas, and she didn't know. But Alex and Jennifer looked at her with such happy, hopeful faces that she could not avoid answering.

"You guys are ganging up on me, aren't you? The thing is, that's a whole year away."

"Aw, come on, Mom," Jennifer interrupted. "You know you've had a good time while we've been here."

Judith couldn't help glancing at Charles. "Yes, I have," she admitted softly. "But who knows how we'll feel come next winter," she added, turning back to her daughter.

The disappointment on Jennifer's and Alex's faces was immediate, and Judith felt a terrible sense of guilt. Who was she trying to fool? The truth was, she'd rather spend next Christmas—and all the ones to follow—here with her family than anyplace else on earth. Why couldn't she admit it?

She swallowed hard and forced a smile. "You don't have to look so glum," she said, deliberately avoiding Charles's searching look. "If nothing interferes with it, we can have Christmas here next year. That is, assuming your father's banker will let us use his house again."

"Yes!" Jennifer shouted.

"And we can invite the Walkers?" Alex asked with an expectant smile.

"Of course," Judith conceded. Then, unable to help herself, she peered cautiously at Charles.

She'd expected to find a triumphant grin on his face, but to her surprise—and vast confusion—he appeared more relieved than anything else. He stared at her as if trying to see right through her. Then he gave her a faint, wavering smile and mouthed the silent words *Thank you.*

Judith averted her eyes at once, blinking back a rush of sudden tears. She was a hopeless optimist and a ridiculous romantic, she decided. A combination that was certain to prove her the fool once more. Yet she could not deny the happy resignation her agreement had generated in her heart. She would try. For another year she would give this marriage her all. Only she wouldn't make it easy on Charles this time. He would have to meet her at least halfway.

"Here, Mom. This is for you and Dad. Open it together," Alex said, giving them a sheepish grin. He thrust a small package into her hand, one clumsily wrapped in tissue paper with red curling ribbon. He ducked his head when she stared at him, so she turned toward Charles.

"Shall we?"

He moved to sit next to her on the couch. "Go ahead. You open it."

Jennifer and Alex watched anxiously as she tore the paper off. When Judith held up the precisely carved wooden ornament, the two children sat back, obviously pleased by the dumbstruck expressions on their parents' faces.

"Oh, my. This is truly exquisite," Judith managed to whisper past the huge lump that had formed in her throat. She held up the ornament by the ribbon tied to it and watched it twist back and forth in the air. It was a cluster of mistletoe—berries, leaves, and branching stems all intricately fashioned to look very realistic.

"You carved this?" Charles asked, staring in amazement at Alex. At the boy's proud nod, he shook his head in wonder. "This is incredible, Alex. Just incredible. You have a real talent for this."

"It's the guitar playing," Jennifer boasted, shooting her brother a fond smile. "His fingers are really strong and really sensitive. It makes sense, doesn't it?"

Alex cleared his throat. "I thought, well, we talked about mistletoe yesterday, and it seemed like we ought to have some. So, I got the idea to carve some." He thrust a similar-looking package at Jennifer. "Here. This one's for you. It's not as good," he hastened to add. "'Cause I did it first."

Jennifer's carving was a snowflake, complete with eight identical prongs. "It's beautiful!" she exclaimed. She leaned over to kiss his cheek. "Thanks, Alex. I love it. I'm going to put it on the tree right now. There," she said, once it was hanging in a prominent location. Then she turned to face her parents. "Okay, now you have to open my present."

Judith was already shaken by the overpowering emotions at play in their little family. She bit down on her lip when Jennifer handed her a flat package. "Let your dad . . ." she barely managed to say.

Charles took the gift, then impulsively pulled his daughter close for a tight hug. "I love you, sweetheart. And you too, sport," he added with a heartfelt smile at Alex. Then he released Jennifer and cleared his throat. "Let's see now. What have we here?"

Inside the package was an ordinary spiral binder, but the cover had a lace paper doily glued to it. On the first page was printed in a neat curling script, *A Christmas to Remember.*

Charles glanced up at Judith, and she smiled back at him in bemusement. She turned the page, and read what was written there. "This book is dedicated to my parents and my brother, Alex. Also to our friends, Joe, Marilyn, Robbie, Lucy, and Josie."

"It's a book I'm writing," Jennifer explained. "I'm going to write a story about Christmas and animals and children. I remember what Alex said about writing words that will be remembered forever, and how I remembered the words 'Some pig,' and then so did Lucy. So I decided to write a book that people will really like, and maybe they'll remember something I said in it. And I'm dedicating it to all of you."

Charles thumbed through the first few pages, so laboriously covered with the beginnings of Jennifer's story. "My daughter, the writer, and my son, the musician and wood-carver." He beamed at them, and Judith knew his pride was total.

"Oh, Jennifer," she said. "This is just wonderful. Will you let us read it as it progresses? Or will we have to wait until you finish?"

"Better let us read it all along," Alex advised. "It might be hard to keep motivated on a long project like this without somebody's encouragement."

Jennifer nodded seriously. "You're probably right."

The rest of the gifts were more predictable, and Judith was almost relieved. She was in too emotional a state to take much more. Even then, however, the least little thing seemed to prod her to tears. Slippers picked because they were her favorite color, teal blue. A pound of her very favorite selection of Godiva chocolates.

Their responses to her gift choices were almost as affecting. Alex loved the microcassette recorder that would allow him to record and thereby remember lyric ideas wherever he was. Jennifer squealed with delight to receive a day of luxury at her mother's favorite salon.

"A manicure and a pedicure. A facial!" she exclaimed. "Just like a grown-up."

Though Alex laughed at the idea, Jennifer was unperturbed. "I bet they could even do wonders with *your* hair," she retorted gaily.

"Walking shoes," Charles said, looking up from a box he'd opened. "Is this a hint?" he smiled as he asked Judith.

"I thought you might enjoy walking. As a way to exercise *and* relax." Then she continued on, saying what she'd long thought, but never voiced. "All your activities are so competitive, Charles. Work first, then tennis and racquetball. But walking isn't . . ." She trailed off, wondering why she'd ever thought walking shoes were a good idea.

He frowned slightly. "I guess that means I can't discuss business when I walk, right?" Then he laughed. "Is walking a solitary sport, or can wives come along?"

He didn't wait for a response from her. Maybe he was afraid of her answer, Judith speculated. She couldn't deny, however, the tiny thrill his words gave her. Then he thrust an envelope into her hands. "Here. I hope you like it."

Judith found herself shaking as she fumbled with the envelope flap. Jennifer and Alex were playing with the microcassette recorder, singing snatches of Christmas songs, then replaying the tape at slower and faster speeds. Charles, however, was staring straight at her, watching her with a guarded expression on his face.

The card was not out of the ordinary. The typical extravagent avowals of a husband to a wife during the holiday season, compliments of Hallmark. The words were lovely, and yet she read it with a growing sense of disappointment.

"Read the paper I put in there," Charles prompted her when she looked up at him.

The paper was neatly hand lettered—a series of couplets, she realized.

In January we'll build a snowman together.
We'll keep ourselves warm, no matter the weather.

When February's patron, St. Valentine, visits,
He'll find us so happy, with true lovers' habits.

In March we'll take long lovely walks by the sea,
Or maybe the mountains, it's no matter to me.

Beneath April showers or among May's fresh
flowers,
What counts most is the time we set off as ours.

In June let's go camping along with the kids.
In July how about fishing—

Judith looked up from the poem, hardly able to believe that he had written it for her. Charles, who
struggled to compose a letter on paper. He could dic-
tate into his ever-present recorder with ease, but putting pen to paper was torture for him. Yet here was a
poem he had written just for her. She couldn't disguise the mist in her eyes, or the tumultuous emotions that rose in her chest.

"I'm going to make this the best year of our marriage," he whispered for her ears only. "I mean it,
Jude. Just give me a chance to prove it. We'll do
things together as a family, and we'll do things together, just you and me. I don't mean those social
functions, either, you know, for business purposes.
We can take walks together. Go to the movies. Go out
to eat without inviting anybody else to join us."

Judith could not respond; the lump in her throat
was too big. In that moment, however, she knew she
wanted to try. She wanted her marriage back, and
she would fight tooth and nail to make it work. How
could she ever have considered abandoning it?

A sob broke through, and with a glad cry she threw

her arms around Charles. The card was crushed between them. August and September, and all the other months, were forgotten. She knew they'd find a way to sustain their marriage throughout the year to come. And beyond.

"Aw, aren't they sweet," she heard Alex chuckle. Even through her tear-blurred eyes she could see, however, that he was beaming. Jennifer edged nearer her brother and wiped at her eyes.

"This is the best Christmas we ever had," she said with a teary smile.

"Yes, it truly is," Judith agreed. She pulled back a little and smiled up at Charles. "It truly is."

Chapter

Fourteen

C harles glanced out the window. Alex and Jennifer were cavorting in the snow, making a game out of shoveling a path to the car. Though they had barely gone half the way to the Mercedes, they were having a great time. Even through the double-insulated glass, he could hear their shouts of laughter. It was the most beautiful sound he could imagine.

Then, as he picked up Judith's humming from the kitchen, he amended that sentiment. Judith's contented sounds and their children's happy ones—it was impossible to choose which brought him more joy. How wonderful that he didn't have to make a choice!

With a tranquil sigh of his own, he sat down in the window seat. He had the Walker family to thank for this. A snowstorm; a rabbit; and a slippery road. He hoped their van had not been too damaged. The fact was, he would gladly pay for their repairs—or even buy them a brand-new van. He owed them that much. Only it was unlikely they'd ever accept such monetary thanks.

They were an odd couple. But their hearts were in the right place, and they were terrific parents. That was undeniable. He hoped they had car insurance to cover any damage to their van.

He stared past the children, down the long driveway, white and gleaming from the bright sunlight glinting off the pristine snow. It was deeper than it appeared, higher than Joe's knees, he recalled.

Then he frowned and searched the wide expanse of snow. It had been deeper than Joe's knees. And yet, where were their footprints? He squinted, searching for some sign of their passing, but it was obvious there was no trail through the snow in that direction. The snow was absolutely unmarred.

Had they taken another route?

He tried to remember, but it had been dark, and he'd still been half-asleep. Had they gone out another way? Charles stood up and went to a different window. But there were no trails broken through the snow on that side of the house either.

A sudden chill snaked up his spine. This was very weird. They had left this morning, so there had to be some sign of it. Had it snowed again? But he knew it hadn't, and besides, it would take an awfully heavy snowfall to cover up the passage of five people.

It made no sense. Was he going crazy?

Judith came in from the kitchen with a stack of dishes and bowls. "You're being volunteered to set the table for Christmas dinner," she said. "You can start with these."

"Oh. Yeah, sure." He gave a last puzzled glance out the window.

"Is something wrong with the kids?" Judith asked at once. She hurried to him and peered outside.

"No, no. They're fine," Charles replied. He put an arm around her and pulled her close. "Better than fine, to tell the truth. And so are you."

When she turned her face up to accept his kiss, he forgot all about the Walkers and their footprints in the snow—or lack of them. He had a second chance with his wife. That's all that mattered to him.

They ate just before dusk after watching a magnificent sunset across the snow-tipped treeline. Turkey, dressing, cream of asparagus soup, salad, glazed carrots, and Mrs. Smith's Original Apple Pie. Even eggnog. It was a feast such as Charles had dreamed about. Finer foods may have been placed before him in the past, served by the most famous of chefs. But this meal had been prepared by the woman he loved —and who loved him. Manna straight from heaven could not have tasted nearly so sweet.

"Does anybody want to watch television?" Jennifer ventured, once the last of the dishes were cleared away and the dishwasher was quietly buzzing. Charles started to say no, but she spoke again. "*A Christmas Carol* is on."

Alex looked up from putting his guitar strings back

on his electric guitar. "Hey, that's the story with Josie's 'God bless us, everyone.' Yeah, I want to watch it. How about you guys?" he asked his parents.

Judith smiled. "To tell the truth, that's exactly what I'm in the mood for. Watching old Scrooge do an about-face."

"I guess I've been a lot like Scrooge," Charles whispered to her as they all gravitated to the living room. "But I'm changing, just like he did."

"You're not the only Scrooge," she confessed. "I've been too fixed in my own ways. We're both going to change for the better."

He stroked her cheek gently, and whispered "I love you." Her soft reply and return kiss made his heart soar. As they settled down side by side on the couch, Charles could not help but think that in their own way, Joe and Marilyn and their children had performed almost as dramatic a miracle on the Montgomery family as Dickens's three ghosts had done for Scrooge. Like guardian angels, the Walkers had flitted into their lives and then out again, leaving them forever changed. How he wished he could thank them properly.

The Ghost of Christmas Future was hovering above a terrified Scrooge more than an hour later, when the telephone rang. A jarring, electronic beep, it seemed completely out of place in the calm of their mountain retreat. Charles disengaged himself from his comfortable sprawl with Judith, and hurried toward the sound. It occurred to him that the phone had probably been reconnected about the same time as the electricity. Yet he had not thought to check in with his office even once the entire day. Even though he knew no one would be in on Christmas Day, he could have reached Doug at home. But the thought had never even crossed his mind. Now, the idea that someone was interrupting his Christmas idyll bothered him.

He picked up the phone with undeniable regret.

"Charles! At last I'm getting through!" Doug's voice came booming over the line. "What the hell's been going on up there?"

"And a merry Christmas to you, too," Charles responded dryly. "It's no big deal, Doug. We just got caught in an unexpected storm. We were without electricity and telephones for a couple of days."

"Talk about the worst timing in the world!" the man swore. "All hell's been cut loose over here, and you've been holed up playing Santa Claus."

"What are you talking about?" Charles turned his back on the door to the living room, shutting out the faint sounds of Scrooge groveling before the most terrifying of his three ghosts.

"It's that damned Garrington. Or to be more exact, his damned interfering wife. He's holding fast to her position that our hotel will disrupt a neighborhood that's already struggling to survive."

"Survive? That seedy area? What's to survive? A few mom-and-pop businesses? A few apartment buildings that should have been either demolished or renovated ten years ago?"

"Not according to the Neighborhood Preservation Center. They think the Washington Street Grocery, Krauss's Sweet Shop, and Gagliano's Market are more important than a hotel that will employ over a hundred people. Not to mention all the construction jobs." Doug swore once more in disgust. "You need to get back here right away. We've got to sit down with

Garrington and do some serious negotiating, otherwise Greenmont Center is going to go up in smoke!"

A memory flashed through Charles's mind: their first house on Cleveland Avenue. They'd been a mom-and-pop operation back then. And what was it Marilyn had said about their first home being little more than a shack? But she'd loved it.

"Dammit, Charles, are you listening? If you don't get back here tomorrow, we may lose everything. The whole project down the toilet!"

"Yeah, I hear you, guy. I hear you."

When Charles finally hung up the phone, he did not return at once to the living room. They had to return home first thing tomorrow. There was no avoiding it. Yet he dreaded telling Judith and the children. Things were going so well, but he knew it was still precarious. One wrong step and he could undo everything he'd already gained.

He sat down next to Judith, only giving her a reassuring smile in answer to her inquiring expression. He focused instead on the television.

Scrooge had obviously awakened on Christmas morning, and was growing more and more giddy with his own good fortune. He had a chance to make up for the unhappy and parsimonious life he'd led, and he was doing so with a vengeance. Carrying the largest goose he could buy, he was visiting Bob Cratchit's meager dwelling, asking forgiveness and promising a raise.

When Tiny Tim's final line was delivered, the entire family sat back in satisfaction.

"God bless us, everyone," Jennifer repeated. She clicked the television off and turned toward her parents. "I sure wish Josie was here to say that again."

Alex didn't say anything, but the sympathetic smile he gave his sister made it clear he felt the same.

At that moment Charles was glad the Walkers were gone. Their presence would have made it even more difficult for him to reveal that this vacation had to be cut short. Neither Joe nor Marilyn would have said anything, but they would have looked at him in that way they had, as if they could see all the way through him.

But if they could see inside him, they would know how much he didn't want to end this vacation. The fact was, he didn't have any choice. Too many other people were depending on him.

"Do you think they're home yet?" Jennifer asked. "How far away is Edgard?"

"It's about a three-hour drive in good conditions, honey. Probably more than twice that long today, though. But they must be home by now," Judith reassured her. "Assuming their van was okay."

"You know, it's been a long day," Charles said. "You guys about ready to turn in?"

Jennifer let out a huge yawn. "I think I'll get ready for bed. But I'm going to work on my book for a while before I go to sleep."

"Yeah, I think I'll go play a little guitar, then turn in, too." Alex rose and stretched before reaching for his guitar. "Good night, Mom. 'Night, Dad." He bent to kiss his mother, and then leaned over unexpectedly to hug his father.

Charles was too taken aback—and too moved—to do more than murmur an awkward reply. After Jennifer kissed both her parents, the two children disappeared up the stairs.

Judith nestled more comfortably against him. "Those are some kids, aren't they?"

Charles nodded, fearing his voice was not steady enough to respond. He tightened his arm around her shoulders. Alex's affectionate gesture only made what he had to do more difficult. He took a steadying breath, aware of the lemony scent of Judith's hair. She'd used a lemon rinse in her hair for as long as he could remember. No matter where he was or what he was doing, the smell of lemons invariably made him think of her. He wondered if she knew that.

"Was that Doug on the phone?"

"Yes."

He felt her wry chuckle. "Was he frantic? This is no doubt the longest time you two have gone without talking business in all the years you've been together."

Charles swallowed. He had to tell her.

"As a matter of fact, he *was* frantic," he began. "There's some problem with the demolition permit."

"There's always bound to be some problem with a project of that size. But let's not talk about business right now." She moved slightly, nuzzling her face against his neck. "We're on vacation. There must be something more interesting we can talk about. Any ideas?" she teased, as she kissed his throat softly.

Charles steeled himself. It was useless to put it off. That would only make her angrier later.

"Jude, there *is* something we need to discuss. About business," he added. He felt the slight tensing of her body, and he heard the intake of her breath. There was a pause.

"What?" she finally asked in a cautious tone.

"I have to go back. Tomorrow. There's a major

glitch," he hurried on, as he felt her rising tension. "We could lose the whole project. A year and a half of planning down the drain. A fortune in fees to architects and a dozen other consultants." He held her tighter when she started to pull away. "I know you're disappointed, Jude. But I'll make it up to you. I promise. I meant what I said in that card. I'm going to make time for all of you from now on." He was babbling, he realized, and it wasn't going to help. With a sinking sensation in the pit of his stomach, he stopped talking.

Judith pushed away from him to sit straight on the couch. She didn't shrug off his arm on her shoulder, however, and he tried to find some reassurance in that. But when she faced him, he knew he was grasping at straws.

"Why can't Doug handle this?" she asked in a voice that sounded too controlled to be natural.

"It's a political problem. Doug's weakness. My forte."

"Your forte," she said after a moment. "Yes, I would have to agree that the politics of business is definitely your forte."

The flatness of her tone alarmed him. "Judith, if I could do it from here by phone, I would. But the situation is too critical."

"What about *our* situation? I think it's pretty critical too."

"We'll go somewhere for New Year's, I promise you—"

"But only if business permits, right?" She stood up abruptly and moved toward the stairs. Then she turned and faced him. "Your forte is the politics of business, Charles. You're very good at it. If you would only put half the thought and effort into the politics of your family life—" She broke off, pressing her lips together. Her hands were clenched into fists at her side. "*You'll* have to tell the children. I have no intentions of making excuses for you. Not ever again."

She started up the stairs, then paused. "Be sure to turn off the Christmas tree lights." Her voice was soft and held a note of infinite regret. Then she disappeared from view.

only put half the pressure that...

Chapter Fifteen

D amn, but it was a hell of a thing when your family refused to understand, Charles fumed. Everything he did, he did for them. None of them had even wanted to come on this trip. He'd had to force them. But they had conveniently forgotten that. Now they were all mad at him because they had to leave early. He couldn't win, no matter what he did.

But Charles did not give voice to his irritation. When Jennifer shot him an accusing look, he only forced a smile. When Alex roughly shoved his mother's pullman bag back to make room for his guitar case, Charles simply leaned forward to straighten the suitcase and settle the guitar case more securely in the trunk of the car. Alex was back to sullen glances and indecipherable muttering, words not meant to be heard by his father but nonetheless clearly conveying his anger.

And Judith. She was dressed and ready to go, wearing a false air of cheerfulness that only made the situation more depressing than ever.

The phone rang and Charles hurried for it, aware that both of the children were glaring at him.

"The meeting is set for three at Garrington's office," Doug informed him without benefit of greeting. "Will you be able to make it?"

Charles sighed and ran a hand through his neatly combed hair, unwittingly leaving it standing on end. "We're leaving now. The morning news said all the roads are open. Even though it will be slow going, we should be there in time."

"We? You planning on bringing the whole family straight to the meeting?"

"No, no. Of course not. It was just a slip of the tongue. *I'll* be there in time. They'll drop me off and you can give me a ride home afterwards."

"Good. I'll see you there." Doug hung up.

For no particular reason, that brief conversation stayed with Charles. They closed up the house— making the beds up with fresh linens, cleaning out the fireplace, emptying the refrigerator of perishable foods. Charles checked the doors and windows, turned down the thermostat, and closed the curtains. Yet even as he pulled the front door closed, locked it, then turned to follow his family to the big automobile, he couldn't get the conversation out of his head.

He'd said *we*, but he'd meant *I*. He always kept business separate from his family, or so he thought. Yet he was only now beginning to see that business always infringed on his family life. He was the one going to that meeting with the wishy-washy Garrington, yet his whole family was being affected. Their entire Christmas was being ruined. It was as he'd said to Doug, not *I*, but *we* would be there in time.

A weary sigh escaped him and he rubbed his eyes. He'd spent a nearly sleepless night just thinking, and even then he'd come up with no solution. Judith had slept with her back to him. In the morning the children had been disbelieving at first, then furious. Yet what choice did he have? He could only cling to the knowledge that he would somehow make it up to them. Maybe he could surprise them with a trip to Disney World—if he could get things settled with Garrington in time. If not . . .

"I'm hungry," Jennifer complained from the backseat as Charles negotiated the snowy driveway and approached the highway.

"I told you to eat breakfast," Judith reminded her daughter. It was the first thing she'd said since they'd started packing the car.

"How about if we stop at that grocery store?" Charles suggested. "We can load up on snacks for the drive home."

There was only silence from the backseat, but Charles took it as agreement. Still, he could not help being troubled. On the surface his family's discontent with him was no different than it had been on the way up to the mountains. They'd gotten over it then; they would get over this, too.

Yet somehow this was much worse. For those few days they'd been so happy. The loss of that happiness now was devastating. He clenched the leather steering wheel and blinked back an unexpected stinging in his eyes.

"Watch out!"

Charles veered sharply to the right at Judith's cry, just missing a bright orange cone placed in the middle of the road. He braked when he saw the tow trucks and the highway police vehicles that were parked at the edge of a sharp drop-off.

"What happened?" Jennifer asked, sitting up straighter in her seat.

"Somebody must have crashed," Alex said sarcastically. Then his tone changed. "Hey, you don't think the Walkers . . ."

"Mom?" Jennifer unfastened her seat belt and reached forward to put her arms around her mother. "It isn't *them*, is it?"

Charles felt an ominous shiver up his spine as they slowly inched past the cordoned-off area. But he shook it off. "No. They were heading in the other direction. Remember? They were headed to Edgard. That's in the opposite direction. Anyway, their van didn't go over the edge. They said it was stopped by a tree."

"Yeah. That's right," Alex said with a pronounced sigh of relief. "I wonder where they are right now."

"They're safe in their own home," Judith reassured them. "No matter how they got home, whether in their own vehicle or someone else's, they're okay. We should be worrying about the people in the car that *did* go over the side."

The ride was very quiet after that, but it wasn't

a sullen, angry silence any longer. It was more thoughtful. Yet Charles couldn't shake the eerie feeling that something was not right. He drove hunched over, squinting into the bright reflection off the snow and holding on to the wheel so tightly that his hands hurt. When the Ruddington General Store finally came into view, he was enormously relieved.

The parking lot was nearly deserted. Only one car and a solitary pickup truck were parked in the partially cleared area. The snow had been pushed back, and now it encircled the parking lot like a thick white fence. Beyond the fence, the forest waited, dark and shadowed in the sunlight, layered still with a blanket of pristine snow.

He parked near a frozen-over watering trough and for a moment they all just sat there. Charles had to force himself to move.

"Okay, time is short. Let's get what we need and get going again."

Outside the silence was absolute. No wind rustled the trees. No birds flitted about. It was too cold for the snow to melt and drip. The dull thuds of the car doors slamming, and then the squeaking crunch of their boots in the snow, were the only sounds to be heard.

Inside, the store was much as it had been four days earlier. The Christmas decorations were still in place, and it smelled of wood smoke and bayberry candles. Alex and Jennifer ambled over to the snacks. Judith picked out a six pack of fruit juices. Out of habit Charles picked up some breath mints and the local newspaper. In less than five minutes they were back in the car.

"Put on your seat belts," Judith instructed the chil-

dren. "Who wants apple juice? Charles, let me pass
out everything before you pull onto the highway.
That road is really dangerous today, and I don't want
anything to distract you."

Their eyes met for a moment, and Charles recognized the worry on her face. The accident they'd
passed had them all upset. He nodded and adjusted
his own seat belt. Then he started the car and just let
it idle.

Once everyone was situated, Judith sat back. "I
think you should finish your juice before you start
driving."

"Don't worry, Jude. I'll be extra careful today." But
he could see she was still edgy. "Here, take a look at
the paper. That might take your mind off the road."

With a sigh she did as he said. Alex and Jennifer
sat quietly in the backseat, eating their make-do
breakfast. Charles was silent, too, as he forced the
apple juice and doughnut down.

Then Judith gasped. "Oh, my God!"

When he looked over at her, her face was white
with shock, and the paper was trembling in her
hands. He frowned in concern. "Judith? What is it?"

"Oh, my God," she whispered again. Then she
turned to face him, and he saw the tears in her eyes.

"What's wrong, Mom?" Alex asked. Jennifer leaned
forward in apprehension.

"It can't be true. It can't," Judith mumbled, shaking her head. "Oh, Charles . . ."

Truly alarmed, Charles grabbed the thin rural
newspaper from her. He searched the page, looking
for he knew not what. Then his eyes stopped at a
moderate-sized headline in the lower left corner:

FAMILY OF FIVE KILLED ON RUDDINGTON HIGHWAY.

Charles's heart stopped in his chest. It couldn't be! But he forced himself to read on. Then he fastened onto one fact and drew a shaky breath of relief. "It's not them. It can't be. See?" He thrust the paper at Judith. "See? It says they were found two days before Christmas. Two days! It was someone else, Jude. It was someone else."

"Daddy? What's the matter? You're scaring me," Jennifer said through her frightened tears.

Alex snatched the paper and found the article. "A car wreck? But it doesn't say who they are," he whispered. Then his voice broke. He looked up at his father and Charles saw the tears well up in his horrified eyes. "They were—" Alex took a harsh breath and the tears spilled over. "They were in a yellow van."

Charles shook his head. "That can't be true. No. It can't. These people here were found days ago." He grabbed the paper back from Alex. "Look. This paper is dated December twenty-fourth. The Walkers were with *us* on the twenty-fourth. There's no way it's them."

Judith looked at the date as well, and he saw relief flood her face. But Charles was perversely not at all reassured by his own reasoning. The same eerie feeling he'd had before came over him again, like an icy finger drawing down his spine. He suddenly felt short of breath.

"Could the paper be wrong?" Jennifer asked fearfully, wiping at her eyes.

"It *could* be wrong, Dad." Alex looked from his father to his mother, then back again. "Let's go ask the man at the store."

Judith got out. So did the two children. But

Charles sat there in the big luxury sedan, letting it idle while he stared blindly into the snowy woods. He knew, with a certainty he could not deny, exactly what the storekeeper would say. He should have known all along, but especially on Christmas morning. They'd left no tracks in the snow.

He'd seen them walk away, all five of them. But when he'd looked later, there'd been no sign of their passing. It had been as if they'd never existed at all.

Like a fool he'd tried to explain it away. He'd been mistaken about which way they'd gone. He'd still been groggy with sleep. Anything to avoid facing the unbelievable truth.

Yet now it was clear and he was both repelled and drawn to that truth. The Walkers were dead. The very knowledge sickened him, and more than anything he wanted to run away from it, to close his eyes and make it not be real.

But he could not make the truth go away, he realized with painful clarity. Just as he had not succeeded in making the truth about the people he most cared about go away. He'd always refused to see the problems between him and Judith. Between him and his two children. Only now was he beginning to understand how blind he'd been. Now, when it was too late.

Yet it wasn't too late for them. Or was it?

In his mind's eye he saw Marilyn holding Josie. He remembered how he had peered through the kitchen window as Joe had taught Alex to chop wood. And he recalled how Jennifer had looked to Joe for help when her own father had been right there. How consumed with jealousy he had been.

And then there was Judith. All she wanted from

him was more of his time and attention. That was all any of his family wanted from him. His time and attention. For them that was the proof of his love, nothing else.

Was that why the Walkers had come to them—come to him? But was it possible? For if they had died before Christmas as the paper said, then the people they'd shared the mountain house with had been . . . Had been what? Ghosts? Angels?

Charles swallowed hard, unable to quite believe it, yet unable also to deny what was now so obvious. They'd come to help him and his family. And they had, he knew. They had.

He looked up, searching for his family with a new sense of urgency. They were huddled on the porch of the store. The elderly man who worked there was standing beside them. He was shifting awkwardly from one foot to the other while Judith clutched both Alex and Jennifer close to her.

Charles made his way to them at a dead run, unmindful of the uneven snow or the slippery steps. He grabbed them in a desperate embrace.

"It was them," Judith sobbed into his shoulder. "It was them."

"I know," he murmured, his throat thick with emotion. "I know."

"The sheriff, he came by here earlier," the old man said sorrowfully. "I'm sorry, mister. I sure am sorry it was your friends. He said their name was Walker. They were artists."

"They were angels," Charles whispered.

"Are you sure, Daddy? Are you sure they're in heaven?" Jennifer sobbed.

Alex met his father's eyes. "They *have* to be in

heaven. Just like we talked about that time." His eyes swam with tears, and it broke Charles's heart.

"I think . . . I think they were somewhere between earth and heaven when they came to us. I mean . . ." He cleared his throat. "They died before Christmas, didn't they?" he asked the discomfited storekeeper.

"They were found the same night the storm broke. Three days before Christmas."

Charles looked down into Judith's wet face and then at his distraught children. "They came to us afterwards," he began. "I should have guessed, but I ignored all the signs."

"You mean they were angels? Really angels?" Judith stared at him disbelievingly. "But that can't be."

"But it is. It's the only explanation."

"Angels?" Jennifer breathed. Her face brightened as her father's words sank in. "All of them? They were all angels?"

"Our guardian angels." Alex's voice was filled with wonderment. "That's so . . . man, it's so cool."

"But Charles," Judith said, still struggling to understand.

"Come on," he broke in. "Let's get out of here."

He herded them away from the old man, who was beginning to stare at them suspiciously. Charles knew no one else would ever believe this. But then, no one else needed to. For some reason, God had seen fit to send a band of his newest angels to the Montgomery family, and Charles was not about to ignore their message.

At the car they stopped, and Charles looked at his wife and children. Their faces reflected both sorrow and an inability to quite comprehend what had actually happened. For his own part, Charles was just as grief stricken, yet he was at the same time filled with the most glorious new sense of happiness. If he'd not known before what was important in life—which choices were right and which were wrong—he knew now.

"I don't know why the Walkers came to us," he began. "But they did. They died in a car accident before we ever met them. But they spent three days with us at Christmastime."

"They were really angels. They really were, weren't they?" Jennifer marveled. She smiled through her tears. "Lucy and Josie and Robbie. And Joe and Marilyn, too."

"But why?" Alex asked. He had wiped his damp eyes, and now he looked to his father for some explanation.

Charles swallowed. His heart was pounding like a drum, and he felt as if he might explode from the joy that swelled within his chest. "I think they came to help us." He looked over at Judith. "To help us be a family again. A happy family that puts one another first. That loves each other totally. And make no mistake, I love all of you so much. So much," he finished in a whisper.

Judith pressed her lips together. Her eyes swam with emotion. "I love you, too, Charles. I always have; I always will. And you, too," she choked out, hugging her children tight.

"I love you, Mom and Dad," Jennifer whispered, breaking into tears again. "You, too, Alex."

"I love you, too, punk," Alex replied. "I love you, Mom. I love you, Dad."

Charles met Alex's gaze for a long lingering moment. He was almost full-grown, he thought. But he would always be his little boy, the son he loved no matter what direction he chose as he grew up.

"Come on, let's go," Charles said with a tremulous smile. "Get in the car. We're going back to the mountain house."

"We are?" Judith said in surprise. "But what about—"

Charles stopped her words with a kiss. How he loved this woman! And what a fool he'd been almost to lose her. He'd never make that mistake again.

"Just get in the car," he replied to the question on her face. "We have a family vacation to finish."

Charles had no sooner put the car in drive than the car phone rang. With a determined set to his shoulders he steered the car out of the parking lot and turned left onto the highway. It rang again, and then one more time.

"Shall I get it?" Judith asked quietly.

Charles looked at her and recognized the fear on her face. It was no doubt Doug calling. She knew it and she was afraid that Charles would once more be swayed by the needs of his business. But not this time. Not ever again.

"I'll get it," he said with a reassuring smile as it rang a fourth time. Then he took a deep breath and reached for the plastic receiver.

"Hello?"

"Charles? Doug. Listen, how's the road look? I need to know how long it will be before you get back. There're some things we need to go over. I thought we could meet at Hilbert's Restaurant, around the corner from Garrington's office. What time can you—"

"I won't be able to make the meeting," Charles broke in on Doug. "I won't be back until sometime Sunday afternoon, like I had originally planned."

"What! Maybe I didn't make it clear how critical this meeting is, Charles. Dammit, this could kill the whole project!"

"No, you made it clear, guy. But, well, let's just say that keeping my family together is more important to me than this project. Than *any* project."

"What in the hell does your family have to do with it?" Doug demanded.

Charles looked at Judith. He saw the beautiful smile that was spreading across her face, and the love that shone in her eyes. He could hardly speak for the powerful emotions that rose in his throat.

"My family has everything in the world to do with it. Everything," he added almost reverently. Then he cleared his throat. "Good luck at the meeting, Doug. I've got to go now, but I'll give you a call when I get home. Oh, and Doug? Merry Christmas, guy. To you and Cora. Do something special for her, okay?"

He clicked off the phone and heaved a huge sigh as he hung it up.

"Way to go, Dad," Alex said from the backseat. Charles met his son's eyes in the rearview mirror and saw the happy grin on his face. He gave him a wink and felt thrilled inside when Alex returned it.

The phone rang again and he glanced at Judith.

"Would you do me a favor, Jude? Hit the control that rolls down the window on my side."

She stared at him, clearly perplexed; then, as the

phone rang again, her mouth dropped open in comprehension. "Charles, you can't mean to . . ."

"Oh, yes, I can." He gave her a look that mingled all the love and hope he now felt, and the terrible regrets he had for the past. "I should have done it long ago."

The electronic ring broke in mid-cycle as he picked up the expensive phone. Doug's voice came out, small and frantic sounding as Judith slid the window down on the driver's side of the car. Then Charles heaved the phone out the window, letting it sail over the edge of the road to land somewhere far below in the snow-shrouded forest, and the connection was broken.

"I think we're going to need more wood when we get back," Charles said conversationally to his son. "I used to chop wood for my grandparents when I was your age, but I might be a little rusty after all these years. Maybe you could give me some pointers."

Alex grinned at his dad, and then at his mother and sister. "Sure, Dad. Anytime."

And now, here's an opportunity to enjoy an excerpt from the same book Judith Montgomery read: *Night Vision* **by Deborah Nicholas, coming from Dell in April 1993.**

A thought suddenly occurred to Simone. "You don't . . . don't think I'm crazy, do you?" She bit her lip anxiously. She was acting like she was crazy, that was certain.

"Crazy?" Mark smiled. "No. Just a little unsettled perhaps."

She winced. "Unsettled" sounded an awful lot like "crazy" to her.

He poured himself a gin and tonic, then came around the bar with both drinks. He sat down beside her on the couch and handed her the Tequila Sunrise. "Actually I'd say you're more than a little unsettled."

She didn't answer, but took a big swig of the drink. The liquor burned pleasantly down her throat. "That's good," she murmured, then let her head drop back onto the couch and took another sip.

After a moment's silence he asked, "Who tore up the upholstery in your car?"

She swallowed another gulp for courage. Should she tell him the truth? She looked at her hands, which still shook. These same hands had destroyed her car; these same hands might be capable of worse things if she didn't clear her head somehow.

Perhaps it was time to tell Mark the truth. Perhaps if he knew everything, he'd stop browbeating her once and for all, and she could put the nightmares behind her.

She lifted her eyes to his. "I did."

He masked his surprise fairly well, although he took a big gulp of his own drink. After a short pause he asked, "Why?"

She gave a shaky little laugh. "Maybe I *am* crazy," she offered.

He slid closer and took her free hand in his. "I don't think you're crazy. But something has upset you. Do you mind telling me what?"

The way he asked the question, allowing her to retreat gracefully, affected her more than anything he'd said until then. She closed her eyes and gripped his hand, clinging to the odd comfort it offered from the vestiges of her nightmare.

"I—I have dreams," she said in a monotone. "They're very real." That somehow seemed inadequate to describe what she'd been going through, so she began again. "I have nightmares. About the Olivers."

His hand tightened convulsively on hers, and she opened her eyes in surprise. But his shuttered expression told her nothing of what he was thinking.

"What kind of nightmares?"

Simone shivered and turned her gaze away. She set her drink down on the coffee table in front of her as she wondered how to describe her private hell.

"Awful, wretched nightmares," she whispered. "I dream that the Olivers are drowning. But it's more than that. They cry for me to help them and I can't." She gripped his hand, remembering. "It's . . . I can't describe how ghastly it is. There's water everywhere and screaming and . . . and today there was blood. Worse yet, they look at me, begging me to help them . . . and their eyes . . . oh, Lord, their eyes haunt me for hours and days afterward—"

She broke off with a shudder, turning her gaze to him in a silent plea for understanding. His eyes filled with sympathy. But they also regarded her with unsettling intensity.

Oh, no, she thought, *he really does think I'm crazy.*

Her control broke then. The first tears slid silently down her cheeks, but before she knew it, she was sobbing aloud.

Mark's pity turned to alarm as he set his own drink hastily aside. "Don't cry, for God's sake," he murmured hoarsely. Nonetheless he pulled her into his arms. "I'm terrible at dealing with crying women," he muttered against her hair.

"I—I'm sorry," she stammered. She wiped her eyes with her fists as if that would stop the tears, but they just kept coming. "I'm not usually the kind . . . of woman who . . . who dissolves into tears at . . . every little thing."

"This isn't a little thing, is it?" he told her in a soothing tone. She shook her head, and he drew her closer still. He said little, but his arms encased her in a cocoon of warm strength. And life. After the numbing fear of her dreams, his body pressed to hers was like a gift of life. It did more to dispel the memory of her dream than even the tears did.

Her tears came more slowly after a while, but he continued to stroke her back over and over, apparently unconcerned that she had soaked part of his shirt where her head was tucked against his chest.

After the first storm of tears abated, she began to be more physically aware of him. The spicy scent of his musk aftershave filled her senses, wiping away the remembered smell of acrid water. And his breath against her hair was so warm, his heartbeat so reassuringly even.

She couldn't deny it. There was something infinitely comforting about being held by a man.

She sighed and rubbed her damp cheek against his chest. The pace of his heartbeat seemed to quicken as he drew her closer still. Then she realized with a shock that her heart was beating a little faster too.

She pulled away, disturbed by her own reaction. He let her draw back, but one of his hands continued to hold hers.

"Thank you for listening," she whispered, unable to meet his eyes.

He lifted his other hand to cup her cheek. "Anything to keep my authors happy," he said with a soft smile, then dropped his hand to hers.

For some reason his words didn't irritate her, but they did remind her of why she'd come. She met his gaze squarely. "Now you understand why I've got to stop writing about the Olivers. The nightmares won't end until I do. And I can't endure the nightmares."

He looked away from her, clearly choosing his words with care. "Have you considered talking to someone about this? A professional?"

She swallowed. "You mean like a shrink? I told you, I've never been to one. I . . . I never wanted to. It's funny. I've never told anyone about the dreams until now. I couldn't find the words."

His jaw tightened. "I see." His gaze swung back to her, a question in its depths. "You know, you still haven't exactly explained how your seat got so torn up."

A weary sigh escaped her lips. It looked like she'd have to tell him all of it. She hesitated before speaking. "Right after I left you at lunch I drove to the lake front. There's a spot I go to on Lakeshore Drive when

I need to think. It's where I first conceived of the Olivers."

She paused, but he didn't respond, so she glanced at him. He watched her, an odd, furtive expression on his face.

"Anyway, I went there today," she continued. "Usually it's so peaceful, I relax easily. Today I fell asleep. While I was asleep, I . . . I . . ."

"You had the nightmare," Mark finished for her.

"Yes. It was totally unexpected. I've never had one while I was at that spot on the lake. My thoughts are generally peaceful." She sucked in a deep breath. "I guess it was because of our discussion this morning."

She looked at him, unable to keep the accusation out of her expression, but he didn't react to it. He merely continued to observe her, a glint of keen interest in his eyes as he waited for her to continue. It annoyed her, this patient silence of his. It was as if he were on the alert for her to let some great secret slip.

She bit her lower lip, then stared off into space, unable to bear those green eyes on her. "The dream is so very real. I usually have it in my own bed and wake up to find that I've thrashed around pretty wildly in my sleep. I—I guess I'm fighting. You see, toward the end of the dream, I . . . I start drowning along with the Olivers."

That seemed to shake him a bit. When she glanced at him she saw he was clenching his jaw, as if to keep from showing what he felt. But behind his eyes gleamed a hint of some darker emotion she couldn't decipher.

"It's pretty horrible," she whispered.

He nodded. "I imagine it would be," he said in a

strained tone. "It seems a rather high price to pay for having a good imagination."

"That sounds just like something my mother would have said."

Her words brought a faint smile to his lips and the sarcastic answer, "Thanks a lot."

She hastened to explain. "Mother always thought I had an overactive imagination. I suppose she was right, but this is different. I mean, I've had some pretty vivid ideas for scenes and stuff, but I've *never* experienced anything like these nightmares. *Never.* My other books didn't do this to me. It began happening only with my latest novel."

Apparently he found that statement very interesting. His eyes narrowed, and he seemed momentarily lost in thought.

She went on quickly, determined to impress upon him just how real the dreams had become for her. "There's more. Today I fought back." She attempted a smile. "I must have grabbed the knife that I'd been using to cut cheese and . . . and tore the seat covers up in my sleep."

A quick image of torn upholstery wiped the faint smile from her face.

He arched both brows. "In your sleep?"

"In my damned sleep," she said with a lump in her throat. "I—I vaguely remember fighting with a weapon against whatever was pulling me down in the dream. I suppose I was doing it in reality as well."

"I'll be a son of a bitch," he muttered, tension evident in every line of his face. He shook his head in mute disbelief. "That's a frightening tale. If I hadn't seen the seat myself, I might have had trouble believing it."

"I guess it does sound incredible." It sounded incredible even to her. What he made of it, she was afraid to guess. She shot him a wary glance, then took a deep breath before plunging on. "One positive thing came out of it, though. It helped me make my decision firm."

At that he released her hand and leaned back. His expression was thoughtful, but she sensed he had somehow slipped back into the suave business persona he'd projected at lunch. "I can see where an experience like that would upset you," he began carefully. He paused as he chose his words. "But that doesn't mean you have to quit a career you love because of it."

His words stunned her. How could he say that after everything she'd just told him? The arrogance of the man! "Didn't what I just said mean anything?" she snapped.

A grim expression on his face, he fixed her with a fierce gaze. "Yeah. Yeah, it meant a lot. It told me that you haven't resolved some things in your mind. But instead of fighting to resolve them, you're running away."

Tension knotted her insides. "You have some nerve telling me that," she hissed. "You don't know what it's like having your mind taken over by something you made up. I bet you've never ripped a seat cushion to shreds in your sleep!"

"No. But plenty of people have played games with my mind, and that's what this is. A mind game. You don't know why you're caught in it, you don't even know what's causing it, but you could find out. Tell me something. You were a cop. Did you ever run from a fight? Did you ever hand your gun over to a criminal and say, 'Here, shoot me'?"

"Of course not! But this is different!"

His eyes glittered like shards of bottle glass. "Is it? Your mind is your gun. You shoot your novels, your ideas, into the world and make people listen to you. And, boy, do your readers listen—millions of them. You hit a lot of them with those ideas, whether you realize it or not. That's why your novels are so popular. They're not just escapist tales. They're philosophy and social history. They're ideas. They affect people."

Simone stared at him in speechless surprise. She hadn't realized he'd read her books, much less really understood or appreciated them.

"And now something is trying to take your gun away from you," he continued, his eyes burning with intensity. "Maybe it's a fear of failure or maybe it's just your creative juices working in a direction you don't want to pursue. But whatever it is, you don't have to give in to it. You *shouldn't* give in to it. Your only weapon as a writer is your mind. You can't just surrender it to the enemy."

What he said made more sense than she cared to admit, but she resisted his logic. "How can I fight when I don't know what I'm fighting? I've never had this experience before. Never. I don't know how to cope with it."

"Why did you leave the police force?"

The abrupt question put her on her guard. She colored. "What has that got to do with this?"

"Why did you leave?" he persisted.

"You heard the interview. I didn't like dealing with corpses."

"You didn't like the smell? The blood bothered you? The idea of death destroyed your illusions of immortality? Be specific, Simone. Why did you quit?"

She didn't want to think about it, but the moment she did, she knew he'd guessed a truth she hadn't even acknowledged until that moment.

"Mind games," she said in little more than a whisper. "Every time I saw a body, I . . . I could imagine the death. Mom always said I had an overactive imagination, but I never really believed it until I became a cop. Then I discovered that my mind would make up scenes for me." She grimaced. "As if the real crime scene wasn't grisly enough. But my good old imagination worked overtime to present in full color what had come before. With only a few details my mind would conjure up the last moments for me, complete with blood. I could even . . . I could even feel how victims must have felt when they were dying. I —I got so I couldn't answer any call to the scene of a homicide."

"Mind games," he agreed. "You ran away then, too, didn't you?"

She threw her head back and closed her eyes. "Damn you. You go for the throat, don't you?"

"Yeah. If I have to. And if what I'm fighting for is worth it. Your books are worth it. *You're* worth it. You're a brilliant writer with the ability to envision tales more clearly than most people. You could embrace that talent, but instead you try to avoid it."

"I'm trying to keep my sanity," she said through gritted teeth.

"You have ghastly nightmares. That's an awful thing—I'm not denying that. I'm just saying you shouldn't let the nightmares stop you from doing what you want to do. And it *is* what you want to do, isn't it?"

She swallowed. She could lie to him, tell him that she was really just tired of writing. But they'd gone beyond the point of lies. He'd never believe her. She sighed, then nodded. "Unfortunately, it's all I ever really wanted to do."

"Then fight it with the weapons you have at hand. Have you ever tried writing the dream down? Putting it into words?"

Her eyes flew open. She'd never thought about it. "What good would that do?"

He ran his fingers through his hair. "I don't know, but it's something to try, isn't it? If you won't see a therapist, and you don't really want to give up your writing, it might be one way to work through your fears."

Simone reminded herself that he wasn't saying all this out of the kindness of his heart. He had a stake in what she did and would no doubt do whatever he could to ensure things went his way.

"What if you're wrong? What if I confront my fears and lose my sanity in the process? You won't care. All you care about is getting my blessed novels out on the shelf so you can make more money off me."

His eyes hardened. A muscle worked in his jaw. "So we're back to that now, are we? All right. Have it your way. We'll talk about what's in it for you, so you won't feel taken advantage of by the ruthless corporate raider. I'll make you an offer. Try my approach. Write one more novel for Pandora to finish out your contract. If my approach doesn't work, if you still insist you can't hack it, I'll release you from the contract. I'll even let you keep the advance."

She looked at him with skepticism.

"I'll put everything in writing, don't worry," he bit out. "But if you complete the contract, I'll not only make good on my promises about having Stance film your novels, I'll quadruple the advance they already paid you for this novel."

She stared at him, stunned. Her previous advance had been very good, so what he offered was a great deal of money, more than she could have expected even if she'd changed houses. It suddenly struck her that his obsession with having her complete her contract seemed to go beyond money, particularly in light of everything he offered.

"Why is it so important to you?" she demanded. "Why are my books so important that you'd offer more money than Pandora can possibly afford to make sure I keep writing?"

Mark looked away startled, then disturbed. Staring off across the room to where a picture window gave a full view of the lake, he sighed. "I want to make Pandora a successful publishing house, and I need your books to do that."

His answer didn't satisfy her. It merely raised another question. "Why did you buy Pandora at all? From everything Tom told me, your computer business is very successful. Why go into publishing when it's such a risky field?"

He met her gaze. "My old business got too comfortable. I needed a challenge, and this was it."

His shuttered expression put the lie to his words.

"That's not all there is to it, is there?" she persisted. "I've told you my reasons for not wanting to write. Now, why don't you be honest with me? Tell me why you bought Pandora. Tell me why you're so determined to convince me to keep writing."

He picked up his drink and stared into the glass for a long time before he finally spoke. "Pandora needed me, so I bought it" was all he would say. Then he added in a husky voice, "And you have to keep writing because the Olivers are too good to die."

He lifted his eyes to hers, and what she saw in his face frightened her. There was determination . . . and more than a little hint of tormented obsession. She knew he was holding something back, knew it with the instincts of a one-time cop. But she also sensed he wouldn't tell her what it was. Not now. Possibly not ever.

He seemed to have a few demons of his own, and she didn't know if she wanted to see them exposed to the light, not when her own demons were playing havoc with her mind.

He was right about one thing, however—she'd been running from the mind games. Maybe it was time to stop.

She didn't know if she should trust him, yet she couldn't help remembering his gentle way of comforting her. He might be a wealthy man, perhaps even vicious in his financial dealings, but he understood pain, that was clear. And right now she felt the urge to throw in her lot with someone who understood about the nightmares . . . and didn't think she was crazy for having them. It was odd, but despite her nightmare that afternoon, she felt she could trust him to protect her, or at least to teach her how to protect herself.

"All right," she said.

"All right what?"

"I'll do it. I'll finish the contract. I'll write another book even if it means fighting my wretched dreams."

He looked at her without expression for a moment. Then his eyes lit with excitement. "You don't have to do it alone, you know. I'll be in New Orleans for the next few months, overseeing changes to Pandora. You can call me whenever you feel the need to talk."

"Anything to keep your authors happy, right?" she quipped. "Well, just remember that if they find someone murdered in my house because I went nuts in my sleep, you'll regret having made me change my mind."

Mark grinned. "Only if the person you murder is me." He added dryly, "Remind me never to sleep next to you when you have a knife in your hand."

His attempt at levity failed the moment they both realized exactly what he'd implied. Her breath left her and she reddened. She wanted to turn her gaze from his, but she couldn't.

Nor could he, apparently. Something flickered in his eyes, something other than the sympathy for her he'd shown earlier. "But without the knife you're welcome anytime." He said it without a smile, without the usual mocking tone of the come-on artist.

With those few words he shattered the protective wall she'd built between them and replaced it with the promise of intimacy, a promise she hadn't even considered until that moment.

The thought of him pursuing her for more than her novels sent her into a panic. Desire emanated from him, hot and inviting and genuine. She definitely wasn't ready for this. She started to rise, but he caught her arm.

"I'm sorry," he said. "I know that sounded like some cheap line. But I couldn't help saying it. You have a strange effect on me."

Simone met his gaze and found herself incapable of speech. His eyes were green fire, and they promised to burn hotter the longer the two of them sat there.

He didn't play games. It was just like in the restaurant. If he wanted something, he asked for it. And he wanted her. Inexplicably, he wanted her.

Her mouth went dry as she acknowledged that his desire wasn't entirely one-sided.

She skirted that thought quickly. "I don't think—" she began.

He cut her off. "Since I've already blundered once, let me get all the blunders out of the way at one time and ask you what's been bugging me all afternoon. Why did you stare at me when you first saw me in the restaurant, before you even knew who I was?"

She groaned and looked away, now thoroughly embarrassed. Little wonder he'd made such quick assumptions. Still, she had no answer for him, because she didn't know the answer herself.

When she didn't speak he lifted his hand to her chin, turning her head toward him until their eyes locked. "You don't know why either, do you?" he asked, his gaze dropping to her lips. "I suspect that you will someday, and the answer will scare the hell out of both of us."

"You scare the hell out of me already," she blurted out.

His hand stroked downward until it rested on her shoulder. His palm felt warm. Too warm and inviting.

"Why?" he asked. "Because I push you to be what you have the potential to be? Because I won't let you give up?"

Simone leveled her gaze on him. *Because you desire me,* she wanted to say, but instead gave him another answer. "Because you want me to continue writing so badly. And I don't know why."

Mark remained silent for several moments, his hand toying idly with one of her unruly curls. Finally he said, "Sometimes it's better not to dig too deeply into someone's motives. They're almost always elusive to an outsider. Demons are mythical, after all."

Yes, she thought, but even myths were real to the believer.